THE LEGEND OF
BILLY JENKS

Other books by Robert Roripaugh:

A Fever for Living

Honor Thy Father

Learn to Love the Haze

The Ranch

RECOGNITION
FOR THE FICTION AND POETRY
OF ROBERT RORIPAUGH

––––––––––––––– *Honor Thy Father* –––––––––––––––

"There have been many western novels ... but this is the best one I have read for a long time.... Laid in the Sweetwater River Valley of Wyoming the author can make the reader see the valley and the long sweep of range country and feel the cold bite of the wind as it pours down from the Wind River Mountains. His characters and their talk are real. When I had finished the book I felt that I had known them and had seen the drama which unfolded."
~ *Portland Journal*

"In *Honor Thy Father*, Robert Roripaugh takes what would seem to be standard materials (rustlers and cattlemen) and fashions them into an unconventional Western enriched with interesting shadings of character and morality." ~*New York Times*

"Set against the sweeping backdrop of the range wars in Wyoming's Sweetwater Valley in 1889, this story of a family torn apart by differing attitudes toward use of the land is a marvelous novel that stands the test of time. Winner 40 years ago of the Western Heritage Award given by the National Cowboy Hall of Fame, *Honor Thy Father* could win again today, so strong is the writing, so finely drawn are the characters...."
~Candy Moulton, *American Cowboy*

––––––––––––––– *A Fever for Living* –––––––––––––––

"Two themes—an affair between Private Paul Travis and Yoko Hosokawa, a secretary at an army base in Japan, and the men's one-sided campaign against a sadistic camp commander—are central in this poignant, quietly powerful novel that takes place in the mid-1950s. The bittersweet quality of the tragically ended love affair overshadows a story that brings the Japanese setting to life in significant detail and gives solidity to characters and personal relationships." ~*Booklist*

"This ... is a swift, smooth, polished and intensely interesting narrative of the life of an American soldier and his unit ... in post-Korean War Japan. Robert Roripaugh's ear for dialogue is exact: whether his characters are soldiers talking barracks-room vulgarities or Japanese harlots chattering flippancies in pidgeon English, the ring of truth sounds constantly. To this the author adds sympathy and grace." ~*New York Times*

―――――――― *Learn to Love the Haze* ――――――――

"Wyoming poems dominate the book ... rooted in Roripaugh's sensitivity to the land, the weather, the wildlife and the people of the state.... *Learn to Love the Haze* is an impressive ... book of poetry." ~Peggy Simson Curry, *Casper Star-Tribune*

"*Haze* is a Western book, full of sage and chamisa, and both the living West and the West of long ago—of Cheyenne, Arapaho, Shoshone—are present.... I would recommend this book to anyone familiar with Western life...." ~Don Snow, *The Salt Cedar*

―――――――― *The Ranch: Wyoming Poetry* ――――――――

"*The Ranch* is a song of labor and animals and family, of landscape, longing, and exultation. Equal parts requiem and ballad. Read it once to lose yourself. Read it a second time to find yourself filled with beauty." ~Mark Spragg, author of *Where Rivers Change Direction*

"This is a fine piece of work—I 'recognized' many of the people and situations in the poems. The title poem is wonderful, and the book builds to a climax beginning with 'The Last Morning'; those final poems are dynamite." ~Linda M. Hasselstrom, author of *Bitter Creek Junction*

THE LEGEND OF
BILLY JENKS

and OTHER WYOMING STORIES

Robert Roripaugh

with a foreword by *John D. Nesbitt*

HIGH PLAINS PRESS

Copyright 2007 © Robert A. Roripaugh
All Rights Reserved
Manufactured in the United States of America

FIRST PRINTING

10 9 8 7 6 5 4 3 2 1

Cover photograph by
Diana Volk, Sheridan, Wyoming

*The Wyoming bucking horse and rider trademark
is federally registered by the State of Wyoming
and is licensed for restricted use through the Secretary of State's office.*

Library of Congress Cataloging-in-Publication Data

Roripaugh, Robert A.
The legend of Billy Jenks, and other Wyoming stories /
Robert Roripaugh.
p cm.
ISBN 978-0-931271-88-5 (trade paper)
1. Wyoming--Fiction.
I. Title.
PS3568.O72L44 2007
811'.54--dc22   2007003259

HIGH PLAINS PRESS
403 CASSA ROAD
GLENDO, WYOMING 82213

CATALOG AVAILABLE
www.highplainspress.com

ACKNOWLEDGMENTS

"The Legend of Billy Jenks" first appeared in *South Dakota Review*, Vol. 9, No. 4, Winter 1971–72, and was reprinted in *The Far Side of the Storm: New Ranges of Western Fiction*, an anthology published by San Marcos Press in 1975.

"Day of the Eagle" first appeared in *Writing at Wyoming*, Spring 1953.

"Winter Days Are Long: Themes Written by Virginia Shield in Freshman English" first appeared in *Quarterly West*, No. 11, Fall–Winter 1980–81.

"The Peach Boy" first appeared in *The Atlantic Monthly*, Vol. 202, No. 3, September 1958.

"The Man Who Killed the Split-Toed Wolf" first appeared in *The Salt Cedar*, One, 1977.

"The Last Longhorn" first appeared in *Sage*, Vol. 11, No. 1, Spring 1966.

"Leave's End" first appeared in *Writers' Forum*, No. 15, Fall 1989, and was reprinted in *Higher Elevations: Stories from the West*, an anthology published by Ohio University Press/Swallow Press in 1993.

"Morning Flight" first appeared in *South Dakota Review*, 40th Anniversary Issue, Vol. 41, No. 1 and 2, Spring–Summer 2003.

For Yoshiko

Contents

FOREWORD BY JOHN NESBITT   ix

The Legend of Billy Jenks   19

Day of the Eagle   53

Winter Days Are Long   63

The Peach Boy   79

The Man Who Killed the Split-Toed Wolf   97

The Last Longhorn   113

Leave's End   129

Morning Flight   155

Foreword:

REAL WYOMING STORIES

For more than a hundred years since the publication of Owen Wister's *The Virginian*, Wyoming fiction has had an inherent contrast between the outsider's view and the insider's. The outsider view is that of an author who comes to the state, does a quick (or not-so-quick) study, and depicts life in Wyoming in a treatment that not all residents agree with; very often, as in Wister's case, the writer seems to impose an Eastern point of view or set of values upon experience in the West. The insider, who may be a native but is often a transplant, is a person who also studies the ways of the country but presents a vision of life that conveys a sense of its being based on Wyoming as people who live here know it. The interpretation has the feel of having come from within and not having been imposed from without.

This may seem at first to be a provincial prejudice, but when a writer comes into a place and writes what expresses itself as definitive fiction about that place, people who live there have a right to respond. Prior to praising Edith Wharton for having "lived in her subject for forty years," Louis Auchincloss (in an afterword to *The House of Mirth*), states:

> The number of novels written about the fashionable world bears little relation to the number of writers who comprehend it. Authors who would not dare describe a coal mine without having worked in one will not hesitate to have a crack at Fifth Avenue.

The Legend of Billy Jenks

What is good for New York should be good for Wyoming or any other place. Many readers in Wyoming and the West wish that Owen Wister had written more consistently from the inside, as he showed some talent for doing so. But readers in Wyoming take *The Virginian* for better and for worse, accepting it as an early landmark in the state's literature. At the same time, readers reserve the right to assess writers who "have a crack" at them.

In the hundred years since *The Virginian* made its splash, several writers have succeeded at writing from within, and no one has done it better than Robert Roripaugh. In his introductory comments to "The Peach Boy" in this collection, he offers "a belief" that he says he has discussed with many of his students: "If what you know is Wyoming and its life and people, you can write serious fiction about it just as well as anywhere else." Assumed in this defense of Wyoming as a literary subject is the belief that one writes about what one knows.

Although this belief may seem self-evident, not all writers share it. Annie Proulx, in an essay entitled "Writing in Wyoming," which is in *Deep West: A Literary Tour of Wyoming* (an anthology in which she and Roripaugh are the two leading authors), offers a vigorous defense of the outsider's view:

> Is a piece of fiction constructed on such quick-read ground worth anything or merely a caricature, a clichéd précis of the subtler undercurrents of lives in a particular place? Or does the outsider's eye more clearly see the habits and traits, the shape of rock and gully that have become invisible through long association to one raised in the place?

After giving somewhat equal treatment to the "outsider writer" and the "native writer," though with an implied bias toward the former, she goes on to state:

> A pernicious ... influence on the novels published today and on the approach of novelists to the world and human nature is the extraordinarily bad advice given to hundreds of thousands of writers through all stages of their development, with particularly virulent

effect in the formative period of their work. That tiresome and harmful advice is to "write about what you know." ... The advice discourages cultural comparisons, discourages venturing out of one's own street into another part of town. It fails to spark interest in words or languages or turn of phrase.

In recent years, Proulx has become well known as the author of "Brokeback Mountain," a story that was made into the controversial and highly successful movie by the same name. The original text comes from Proulx's collection *Close Range: Wyoming Stories*, the subtitle of which implies a claim that the stories represent Wyoming experience. It is inevitable that the work of Proulx, the quintessential outsider, be compared with the work of Roripaugh, the native writer.

Though he was not born in Wyoming (where being a native confers a status of its own), Roripaugh is a naturalized transplant, and his writing is what Proulx would call native. Born in Oxnard, California, in 1930, Roripaugh grew up in various places in the West and Southwest, graduating from high school in Midland, Texas, in 1947. He spent two years at the University of Texas at Austin, majoring in journalism and geology. Then in 1949, Roripaugh's family bought a small ranch near Lander, Wyoming, in the Wind River country in the west-central part of the state. As he writes in the introductions to some of the stories in this volume as well as in his prologue to his poetry collection entitled *The Ranch*, life on the family ranch for the next several years would leave a lasting influence on him and his writing.

After graduating from the University of Wyoming, the emerging author had two years of military service (1953–55), which included a year in Japan, and then a year in Laramie as a Coe Fellow in American Studies and two years of graduate work at the University of New Mexico. Then in 1958 he moved back to Wyoming to take a job in the English department at the University in Laramie, where he served with distinction until his retirement in 1993. Two years later, in 1995, he was appointed Poet Laureate of Wyoming for a term lasting until December 31, 2002.

In a half-century of writing, Roripaugh has been a versatile author, publishing short stories, poems, reviews, articles, and two novels. *A Fever for Living* (1961) is drawn from his experiences in Japan, and *Honor Thy Father* (1963) is set in the ranch country that Roripaugh has come to know and love. After these two novels came a poetry collection, *Learn to Love the Haze* (1976), which contains an impressive range of poems both personal and regional, and then *The Ranch: Wyoming Poetry* (2001), which draws upon the author's attachment to the family ranch.

Concurrent with the above events in his career, Roripaugh has published the short stories in this collection, beginning with "Day of the Eagle" in 1953 and carrying through to "Morning Flight" in 2003. One common feature of his stories is that they are grounded in and grow out of Wyoming and western experience. Two other common features are those that Proulx grants to all serious writers: "an understanding of human behavior and the driving necessity to write well." The stories contained in this volume will bear out Roripaugh's assertion, quoted earlier: "If what you know is Wyoming and its life and people, you can write serious fiction about it just as well as anywhere else."

The title story, "The Legend of Billy Jenks" (1971), is an ambitious story in technique as well as in content. The narrative voice, which resembles that of Faulkner's "A Rose for Emily," works as a composite voice for the town, as it tells how Billy Jenks comes to have a grudge against the town and dies at its hands. In Roripaugh's story, it is interesting to track the narrator's comments as they progress in tone.

Unlike Faulkner's story, in which the title character is one of the town's own, Billy Jenks is a marginalized young white man who has "Indian blood himself on his mother's side" and who associates with a Mexican named Pete Pacheco and an Arapaho girl named Violet Running Bull. The voice of the story generally reflects a sympathetic view of Billy until he and an accomplice (who everybody assumes is Pete Pacheco) rob the town bank and hole up in the express office. After the bank fiasco, the narrative persona expresses an ambivalence that the events of the story undercut with irony. The townsfolk are plenty eager to arm themselves and ambush a couple of bank robbers, especially when one of the robbers hurls a nasty insult and the other is thought to be a wino Mexican, and then the townspeople do not show much remorse when they discover what they have really done.

Although the story does not encourage approval of Billy Jenks' antisocial behavior, it does elicit sympathy for the underdogs in life—in this case the poor whites who are affiliated with the Shoshones and Arapahos—who fight out their frustrations against the figures of power and authority. "The Legend of Billy Jenks," like other works by Roripaugh, ends with the death of a person who, partly because of his affinity with the darker-skinned races, does not fit in with the established order. However, this story does not constitute a protest against injustice, as the main character brings on the final situation by his own actions. The resolution is what some people would call a negotiated ending, with relative actions of better and worse balanced against one another.

The second story of this collection is, as Roripaugh mentions in his introductory comments, the best of his first early stories. "Day of the Eagle" shows a developing writer exploring technique and subject matter that will appear in later long and short fiction as well as in poetry and nonfiction by the author. This story might remind some readers of Walter Van Tilburg Clark's "The Watchful Gods," in which a young boy goes out alone on the landscape to hunt. As the boy in this story is skinning a bobcat, a girl appears, and like the significant female characters in Roripaugh's later fiction, she has dark hair. The encounter with the girl and their shared experience of watching the landscape and an eagle overhead makes the boy feel "wild and strange, like he was maybe an Indian." The story blends the landscape, its wildlife, the horse, the hay meadow, and the girl into an ideal order in which natural elements, real things of the world, prevail.

"Winter Days Are Long" is a very moving story, and it is always at the top of the list when my own students of Western American

Literature rank the reading selections for the semester. In addition to being an eloquent story in its own right, it shares thematic features with the author's other fiction as well as his poetry and nonfiction. One major feature is a respectful but non-sentimental depiction of non-white people. In Virginia Shield, the reader sees a young Native American trying to find her place in the world as she struggles with the injustice and sadness of the world on and near the reservation. The sympathy shown for the narrator and for her "shadow sister," Michelle Yellowbird, is reminiscent of and more fully developed than the treatment of Violet Running Bull in "The Legend of Billy Jenks." As Roripaugh mentions in his introductory comments to "Winter Days Are Long," it is a companion piece to his poem "Elegy for an Indian Girl"; it is also in harmony with another excellent poem of his entitled "For an Indian Bronc Rider Killed in a Highway Crash Near Ethete, Wyoming," also distinguished by restrained emotion. In addition to being treated sympathetically, Virginia Shield has a symbolic dimension. Like the girl in "Day of the Eagle" and like the Japanese and Native American main female characters in Roripaugh's novels *A Fever for Living* and *Honor Thy Father*, Virginia Shield is characterized by her affinity with nearby fields and meadows and with mountains in the distance, so that she embodies the integrity of the natural world.

"The Peach Boy," written many years before "Winter Days Are Long," connects with the best of Roripaugh's work. Like the novel that would follow, the story is about a main character who is in love with a Japanese woman. As in the earlier "Day of the Eagle," the dark heroine is presented in images that link her to the fertile world of plant and animal life, but in this story the emotion is more subdued, as the protagonist ruminates on a relationship that has ended rather than on one that might yet materialize. The sadness of separation is complicated by the problem of adjustment of the serviceman returning home. This complication might remind some readers of Ernest Hemingway's well-known story "Soldier's Home," in which the protagonist feels pressure from his mother to settle down. Bill Reno's circumstances correlate with other details in the story. The magpies in the chicken-wire trap, which are black and white, suggest the relationship between Reno and Toyako, and they recall the crows outside the apartment in Japan from earlier in the story. This story blends impressions of Japan and of the Western American landscape with the tension of unresolved emotions, all supported by realistic detail with symbolic dimensions. A reading of this story helps one appreciate how its success had such a positive influence on the author's career.

"The Man Who Killed the Split-Toed Wolf" shows thematic continuity with Roripaugh's other stories, from "Day of the Eagle" through "Winter Days Are Long," "The Peach Boy," and others. In addition to being an almost mythic story about a legendary wolf and the man who killed it, "The Man Who Killed the Split-Toed Wolf" is also a story about a young narrator coming to understand the world around him, and especially the mystery of wildness, through the help of a Native American mentor. The man who killed the wolf, Slade Wilson, is a white man who has affinity with native ways, as he lives on Squaw Creek and achieves a great act in the primitive world. Charlie Six-Fingers, whose name suggests a kindredness with the wolf, not only relates the story to the young narrator but also expresses an elemental appreciation of the power of the animal. When Charlie runs his hand along the picture of the wolf and the man who killed it, the story conveys both an elegiac feeling for an earlier era and a deeper feeling of awe for the primitive, all through the gesture of the modern Indian. The narrator has also felt the wonder and has thought that even Slade Wilson might have been "deathly afraid" of the great animal he killed. This story does an excellent job in synthesizing the legend with the medium of the Native American and the growing awareness of the young narrator.

"The Last Longhorn," like "The Legend of Billy Jenks" and part of "The Peach Boy," takes place in a small Wyoming town resembling Lander, which is near the location of the family ranch that has held so much influence in Roripaugh's work. The atmosphere and the characters of the story are very realistic, continuing Roripaugh's success at writing stories set in the real world of his own experience. One aspect of the story that might go under-appreciated by some readers is the non-typical narrative point of view. As Roripaugh mentions in his introductory comments to this story, the narrative point of view is objective. That is, the perspective of the story stays outside all of the characters. This is an interesting technique in support of the theme of the story, as the narrative ends on a somewhat wry, noncommittal note about the tendency of professors to look for material and the willingness of colorful local characters to furnish the stories. Most of Roripaugh's other stories—especially "Day of the Eagle," "Winter Days Are Long," "The Peach Boy," The Man Who Killed the Split-Toed Wolf," and "Morning Flight"—draw emotional power from staying up close to the impressions of the main character. But even within those stories, one finds variation in method, from third-person narration limited to the main character's experience to first-person narration by an observer or synthesizer to first-person epistolary or documentary narration. Add to that the communal narrative voice of "The Legend of Billy Jenks" and the objective voice of "The Last Longhorn," and one has an interesting range of narrative techniques to appreciate in this collection.

"Leave's End" continues another significant thread in Roripaugh's writing, and that is the presence of a Native American protagonist. Supported by a strong sense of place in the ranch country of Roripaugh's writing, the story features a Native American character, who, like characters in earlier stories such as "The Legend of Billy Jenks" and "Winter Days Are Long," has a major crisis as a result of being in conflict with the white community. This story is different from the other two, as John Runner's fate is the direct result of racism. Although this story is sympathetic to the Native American character, it is not as restrained as the two earlier stories or the two elegiac poems "Elegy for an Indian Girl" and "For an Indian Bronc Rider Killed in a Highway Crash Near Ethete, Wyoming." Thus, even within a given subject matter, Roripaugh varies his treatment—all the time, as he says in his comments on this story, writing about the world he knows.

FOREWORD

The last story in this collection, "Morning Flight," in addition to being one of the longer pieces, is also one of the more complex. Set in Casper, Wyoming, during World War II, it is narrated from the point of view of a twelve-year-old boy who yearns to go duck hunting with his father and who also ponders women and the mystery of their attraction. The story presents a well-managed array of details from the war years, and it also offers a finely textured rendition of the world of duck hunting, continued testimony to Roripaugh's masterful use of material from his own experience. Moreover, it achieves a delicate synthesis of the boy's dreams of being a fighter pilot, being close to a woman, and hunting ducks with his father. The story gives a full, well-balanced treatment to each of the boy's preoccupations, and it culminates in a graceful resolution of the conflict between fantasy and reality. This is an emotionally satisfying story about a boy coming to awareness, a nice companion to some of the earlier stories in which young people grow into a sense of the world, and it gives an eloquent close to this collection.

What we have, in sum, is a superb collection of Wyoming stories—real in content, real in emotion, and excellent in technique. As Henry James described it in the 1908 preface to *The Portrait of a Lady*, the house of fiction has many windows; Robert Roripaugh's is but one, and it is a very good one. There is plenty of room for others. Today's reader is under no obligation to choose between "Brokeback Mountain" and "The Legend of Billy Jenks" (which coincidentally take place very close together in time and place), but a person who reads the latter will want to read more by the same author. Thanks to High Plains Press, the reader of this current collection has the opportunity to become immersed in first-rate fiction and real Wyoming stories.

John D. Nesbitt, Ph.D.
Eastern Wyoming College

THE LEGEND OF BILLY JENKS

HEADNOTES FOR "THE LEGEND OF BILLY JENKS"

"THE LEGEND of BILLY JENKS" was first published by the *South Dakota Review* in 1972. Martha Foley listed it in *The Best American Short Stories* as one of the distinguished stories for that year. In 1975 it was reprinted in Gary Elder's anthology, *The Far Side of the Storm: New Ranges of Western Fiction,* which included work by Max Evans, William Eastlake, Frederick Manfred, and a dozen or so other authors writing about the West in nontraditional ways. Although its length made finding a magazine willing to publish the story difficult, the work I did writing it involved aspects of creating fiction about Wyoming life and people that have intrigued me for years.

Like other stories in this collection, "The Legend of Billy Jenks" is set mostly in a small ranching and tourist town close to the crest of the Rocky Mountains and not too far from the Wind River Reservation shared by the Shoshones and Arapahos. The country along the Sweetwater River, settled with large ranches running cattle or sheep, forms the background for this story, as it would for my historical novel set in the late 1880s, *Honor Thy Father.* Billy Jenks' life covers twenty-three years, beginning in 1929 and ending in 1952, but references in the story move back into territorial days and ahead to the state's seventy-fifth year of statehood in 1965. One of the most interesting time periods for me as a writer is the 1950s and early 1960s. These were the years when I began to write and publish fiction dealing with a Wyoming that was sharp and alive in my mind and still remains home.

Despite its length and unlike most of my stories, "The Legend of Billy Jenks" was not difficult to write and revise into final shape. Once I found the point of view and voice, a first-person narrator recalling the events and speaking for the townspeople, the writing began to flow as though I might really know where it was all headed. Telling a story through a narrator representing the town isn't too common in fiction. But it does have the immediacy and apparent reliability that makes first-person storytelling so popular in writing and speaking. In "The Legend of Billy Jenks," the plural viewpoint of the town, as "we," also supplies knowledge of the area's historical and cultural past, the characters, and the events leading up to Billy's defiance of all the people and circumstances he believed had wronged him. When described by the narrator, reactions from residents of the town and its surroundings to Billy's actions and character become essential to the story as it ends.

Did I know anyone who served as the basis for the character of Billy Jenks? Perhaps part of the author is found in almost all of the characters in his or her writing. Billy and I would be about the same age and I too grew up during the Great Depression. Like Billy I worked summers in the hay fields and even spent time hunting, fooling around, and working occasionally out along the Sweetwater, though I didn't shoot anyone's cattle. But like many other fiction writers, I believe my characters are mostly composites of real people and human traits given shape by memory, observation, imagination, reading, and the needs of the story. However formed, they should be believable and reasonably consistent, though capable of changing and sometimes, like real people, surprising us.

THE LEGEND OF BILLY JENKS

When Wyoming celebrated its seventy-fifth anniversary of statehood, Billy Jenks would have been thirty-six years old. Probably Billy wouldn't of paid much attention to the celebrations and speechmaking going on around the state—or to the extra color in the Fourth-of-July parade in his hometown, the stories in the local newspapers about famous early citizens of the area like Butch Cassidy and Jim Averill, and the reenactment for tourists passing through of the lynching of Cattle Kate Maxwell back in 1889 for allegedly accepting her pay from lonely cowboys in calves that belonged to her neighbors out on the Sweetwater.

While the town celebrated on the Fourth, Billy Jenks would of hung around drinking beer by himself in the bars where a few old-timers might still be talking about how Cassidy and Cattle Kate hadn't been outlaws at all, and how taking from the Union Pacific and those foreign cow barons who owned big ranches along the Sweetwater River wasn't stealing. Hell, a man had a right to appropriate enough to live on from rich sons-of-bitches who had been a little shady themselves while putting together their land, money, and power.

That kind of talk wasn't new around town, of course, and most of us had grown up hearing it without bothering to think about whether it was true or fair. After all, there hadn't been much wealth in town—a uranium strike in the county stirred up hopes in the early fifties, but for each of us who made a little money, there were four or five others who went broke—so it seemed right to be scornful of old ranching families like the Rademachers who appeared to have more of everything than they needed. Certainly Billy Jenks would of agreed with the old-timers as they sat around the back booths at the Buckhorn or the Silver Dollar, looking dry and a little shrunken in their town clothes and clean Stetsons, and defended the notorious elements of our early citizenry. He had heard the same kind of talk all his life from his old man or Silas McClintock, who ran a bar and service station where Billy worked for a time before getting sent to the pen.

But Billy Jenks wasn't around in 1965 to celebrate anything or hear the loose-mouthed talk going on in the bars. He was, in a manner of speaking, up on Cemetery Hill east of town, where you can still go to see the simple headstone that reads:

WILLIAM "BILLY" JENKS
1929–1952
Too Young To Die
Too Old To Live

From Billy's grave, unimpressive at first glance in the midst of more elaborate granite markers and memorials, you can see the sawlike spine of the Wind River Mountains to the west, gentler foothills sloping up in tilted tables of sagebrush and mountain cedar, and green-and-yellow swatches of hay meadow and cropland washing down the valley around the town. To the southeast lie the dull grays and tans of range country along the Sweetwater River, the sheep-and-cattle country where Billy Jenks was born just as the "Great Depression" began and only a few years before Franklin Roosevelt was elected president.

Of course Billy didn't grow up among much interest in national politics and whether the NRA was unconstitutional. For Billy's old man and most of us living in town, economics was still a personal problem rather than something connected with how you voted. It was hard enough to live when times were good, and Jack Jenks didn't blame Herbert Hoover or the Depression for his being poor. That was his own fault, he would of said—his being too honest and born too late to put together a sprawling ranch by conveniently using and ignoring the law like he thought the family he worked for, the Rademachers, had done.

A hand-to-mouth cowboy, Jack Jenks was on Old Man Rademacher's payroll mainly to help put up wild hay, build fence, and ride through winter storms to see how the white-faced cattle were getting along. People in town used to say that more often than not the RH stock got along better than Jenks and his family did. The three of them lived in a one-room log house with a tarpaper roof down behind the corrals at the Rademacher headquarters, where the oldest son, Pink, ran things whenever his father, a widower, was staying at the house in town.

Billy was born in that log shack, which had once been a lambing shed before Old Man Rademacher bought out—some described the transaction more harshly—the sheep outfit of a Scotchman named Silas McClintock. The bar McClintock opened on the highway soon became the Saturday-night social center for ranch hands in a fifty-mile vicinity. It was the place where Jack Jenks headed every payday and some Saturday nights in between, leaving his wife and Billy at the headquarters while he bummed a ride in the cook's Model-T or rode over on his bay horse for a session of beer drinking and card playing with the cowboys, sheepherders, and assorted hangers-on who happened to be passing through for one reason or another.

If Rena Jenks objected to her husband's spending the nights and most of his pay at McClintock's, she kept her complaints to herself. She was much younger than Jenks, half-Shoshone people in town would always say when her name came up in a conversation, sleek-haired and a little moon-faced, but still attractive despite the cheap print dresses she made for herself from material purchased at Penney's bargain counter when her husband brought her in to shop once each spring and fall. Before marrying Jenks she had kept house for Old Man Rademacher and his sons, and since Pink hadn't married yet she still helped out at the headquarters from time to time.

The way the story was told around town, by the time Billy Jenks was four or five he should have been used to spending a lot of time playing out behind the shack by himself. His father would eat breakfast with the other hands in the bunkhouse kitchen and spend most of the day working miles away from the ranch buildings. Apparently Billy's mother would leave the shack for several hours each morning and afternoon to do the Rademachers' washing or help out in the kitchen. And often when Jack Jenks had gone to McClintock's after the evening meal, she would put Billy to bed and leave him alone for a long time with nothing to do except listen to the wind crying at chinks in the log walls if it was winter, or watch a long sunset stain the window glass in the summer.

Then one night in December it began snowing soon after Billy's mother had left the shack. There was a moon, and Billy would have been able to see flakes drifting and melting on the window. Footsteps approached the shack, and the door opened noisily.

"Rena?"

At the sound of his old man's voice, Billy sat up in bed, rubbing at his eyes. "She ain't here," he finally said.

"I figured as much." Jack Jenks' shadow didn't move. "You stay quiet there, boy. You hear me?"

Billy was almost six by then, and probably he had learned the hard way to obey things his old man said in that edgy tone he used when talking about money or some shortcoming of the Rademachers. The fire in the stove had burned down, and the boy sat there in the cold, watching his old man's shadow move across by the shelf over the other bunk and then fade into the chair opposite the door, while snow sifted down silently against the window.

The sounds that came later were made by feet stepping lightly in the new snow and the door opening with a shudder because of the cold. Billy saw moonlight on his mother's face as she moved through the doorway. More cold air came into the cabin.

"You just now getting back, are you," Jack Jenks said.

"Yes," she said, still standing in the doorway. "Don't wake the boy."

"I don't suppose it matters, Rena. You surprised to see me?"

"Yes," she said.

Jack Jenks laughed. "I decided to turn back when the snow started up. I guess you been over to the big house again. Nice and warm over there, ain't it?"

She made no answer and her face showed nothing.

"I guessed there might be some truth in what I was hearing," said Jack Jenks. "About you and him.... I knowed better than to trust a man that had everything laid right in his lap by his old man. They got the money and land out here. They can hire a dumb bastard like me for next to nothing to dig their postholes and calve out their damn blue-blooded cows. But that ain't enough. I'm supposed to let Pink Rademacher rut like one of their range bulls with my poor slut of a woman."

Billy's mother had disappeared from the doorway where moonlight now cast a misshapen oblong onto the fresh snow. The boy had to strain his eyes to find her again, a scallop of darkness beyond the other bunk and close to the wall. Then the chair rungs made a sound, and Jack Jenks appeared in front of the window in the yellowish light. He held something dark and shiny in one hand—the worn Colt six-shooter he sometimes called his "equalizer."

"There's one thing the Rademachers ain't got yet, Rena. They ain't got me scared of them. Now I'm going up to the house and find Pink. You and me can settle up after that."

His mother said nothing then ... or afterwards when Jack Jenks had walked through the open door of the shack. She stood pressed up against the wall as though waiting for something, and the boy waited too as more snow drifted onto the worn planks inside the doorway. Finally they heard the first gunshot, sounding loud and close-by in the brittle air, and the boy must of wondered why his mother didn't get undressed for bed now it was all over.

While Billy Jenks was growing up, he acted like he knew all there was to know about what happened that December night in 1934. His old man had "done what he had to do," and his serving a jail term for it didn't seem to lower Billy's opinion of him any. The boy was living in town with his old man's sister and her husband, and if some of the kids at school made the mistake of calling him a jailbird's son, they soon learned better. It wasn't that Billy was big or tough. He just waited until the kid who had taunted him was off by himself somewhere and then went for him with anything that was handy—a piece of two-by-four, somebody's shovel, or a good-sized rock. He didn't make many friends at school, but he wasn't picked on either.

Billy's mother went away right after Jack Jenks' trial, and as far as we knew she never saw her son again. According to the town gossip, she was working as a waitress in a café down in Green River. She would probably come to a bad end down there among the sheepherders and Union Pacific train crews, people said. It was easier to blame her for the trouble Jack Jenks got into, since Pink Rademacher soon married a schoolteacher from Colorado, and that somehow seemed to make him look better. Besides, Pink had a crippled right arm from getting shot with Jenks' forty-five that night, which created a little sympathy of the sort most of us didn't usually feel for the Rademachers. It came out at the trial that Jack Jenks had gotten Pink out of bed in his room at the big house, firing at him and missing. And then they had been wrestling around, with Pink just about getting the cocked Colt away from him when it went off. That was how Pink Rademacher got his gimpy arm, and he had to finish the fight by knocking out Jack Jenks with his left hand.

Billy believed a different version of the story, one where his old man did the whole thing right, and pretty soon the truth about what had happened got all mixed up anyway, since the Rademachers still had plenty of enemies. When Jack Jenks got out of jail in 1936, he didn't have much trouble getting a job, and there were some in town who went out of their way to make him feel nothing was held against him. He rented a room at Mrs. Hamilton's boarding house—Billy was almost eight and still living with the sister—and in a couple of years he scraped together enough money to buy a secondhand haybaler.

The next summer Jack Jenks began contracting baling for some of the smaller ranches in the valley, and in the winters he drove one of the county snowplows. We would see him downtown most every night in the Silver Dollar or the Buckhorn, a thin-mouthed little man who still dressed like a cowboy and drank by himself at the back of the bar near the jukebox. If one of us caught him when he had been drinking heavily enough, he would say what he thought of the big landowners out on the Sweetwater. But he never would talk about Pink Rademacher and his crippled arm.

"You ask him about it," he would say. "I ain't the son-of-a-bitch who brought on the trouble."

For some reason nobody wanted to ask Pink about it....

In the summers when Billy was older, he worked with his old man in the hay fields. They bought a small tractor with a side-delivery rake, and with it the boy would lay the hay into windrows for Jack Jenks to bale. After the big war started in 1941, the local National Guard unit was called up, horses and all, and most of the younger men in town went into the service. There was a shortage of hay-hands, so Jenks and his boy had all the work they could handle. They didn't seem to mind putting in long hours to get a man's hay baled, but Jack Jenks had the reputation for meanness if he didn't get paid promptly once a job was done.

"I ain't got any land or cows like you," he told one rancher who wanted to wait until shipping time to pay for his baling. "This haying machinery is all I own, and nobody's going to stall around about paying me for what the boy and I earn with it. If you want, I can take the cost of baling that hay out of your hide."

The rancher went to the Stockgrowers' State Bank the next morning and borrowed money to pay him.

Then one night just before the war ended, Jenks got into an argument with a roughneck from Oklahoma who worked on a drilling rig out south of the Sweetwater. They had both been drinking all night in the Silver Dollar, and the roughneck, who had lost some money to Jenks the weekend before in a stud-poker game, called him a "cock-suckin' cowboy." Billy's old man went home, got his Colt, and came back to the bar with the forty-five stuck in the waistband of his Levis. When he tried to pull it on the roughneck,

Jenks' thumb slipped on the hammer, and the heavy bullet went down into his groin and ripped all the way through his left leg. A few days later Billy watched his old man die of blood poisoning up in the county hospital.

It wasn't too long after Jack Jenks was buried that we began to hear a lot about Billy. He quit high school after two years, capping off his educational career by laying open the shop-teacher's head with a chunk of plywood during an argument over whether Billy was or wasn't going to take his turn sweeping up after class. He went to work on the town's old yellow trash truck, and all winter we saw him riding up and down the alleys with the cross-eyed driver and a wino Mexican named Pete Pacheco, bareheaded and trying to look warm in his old man's denim jacket.

By then Jack Jenks' sister had left her husband and was living with an ex-bootlegger who ran a honky-tonk several miles out of town on the highway. Billy moved into an old log garage down behind the lumberyard that someone had turned into a rental by boarding up the front and putting in a cast-iron stove. He kept his old man's haying equipment in the vacant lot across the street, and we thought he would take over the custom-baling business in the summer. But instead a new man appeared on the trash truck, and the Jack-Mormon who ran an automobile dealership on Main Street reported that Billy had sold the baler, tractor, and side-delivery rake and bought a new green pickup. Nobody expected him to keep living in the shack now that he had a little more money, but when the pickup was always parked there, people said that kind of house probably made him feel comfortable by reminding him of the patched-up lambing shed his family had lived in out on the Sweetwater.

The summer haying season came and ended, and Billy Jenks still hadn't taken a job. He bought some shells one day from Stillson's Sporting Goods, and someone saw him out at the town dump blasting away at rusty beer cans with his old man's forty-five. The old-timers who had been at Jack Jenks' trial shook their heads, grinning and winking at one another when they heard the story. But the

The Legend of Billy Jenks

town had begun to grow after the war, and the newcomers and some of the older citizens who believed the legend that Jenks had outdrawn Pink Rademacher in the last real gun duel in that part of the country were thrilled and a little worried. That was when people got to calling him "Billy the Kid"—not to his face of course, though he probably knew about it.

By the time Billy Jenks reached nineteen, he was already one of the town characters, which said a lot for him since most of the others who had reached that status were at least forty or fifty. Almost any evening you would see him driving up and down Main Street in his pickup. Usually he would be by himself or with Pete Pacheco, which was about the same thing. When he finally parked and got out in front of one of the bars, he would be wearing a black hat with a bull-rider's crease and the brim carefully rolled, a flowery Western shirt, old Levis, and what everyone assumed were his old man's boots. He wasn't of legal age to drink, but none of the bartenders paid much attention as long as the customer wasn't an Indian from the reservation north of town. Like Jack Jenks, Billy liked the back of a bar and drank by himself.

"Good to see you, old buddy," the bartender at the Silver Dollar said one evening when Billy came in earlier than usual. Actually he had been there for several nights in a row, but Chuck was polite to his customers.

Billy pushed his hat back and gave his old man's thin-mouthed smile. It disappeared quickly into the pale wedge of his pocky face.

"A draw, Billy?"

The boy nodded, and Chuck slid the glass under the tap and leveled off the head with a wood paddle. He set the beer in front of Billy and fingered out fifteen cents from coins the boy had spread out before him on the bar. Except for a booth filled with highway-construction workers with dusty faces and tin hats and a couple of the bar's regulars talking together up front, business was light. Chuck rang up the sale and came back to where Billy sat.

It was October of a long fall with the trees above town in the mountains holding their bright leaves later than usual. Hunters were already complaining that the deer-and-elk season would open without enough snow to drive game down from the high country. A man would have trouble getting his meat unless he knew some rancher who would let him hunt the tamer deer that always hung around haystacks in the foothills close to town.

"Not much going on," Chuck said. "Football team's playing up in the Basin this weekend, I guess. I heard they've got a good chance to win some games this year."

Billy's supply of casual conversation was practically nonexistent. Mostly he listened and sipped his beer. "You seen Pete around?" he finally asked.

"If you mean Pete Pacheco, he hasn't been in," Chuck said. "You want me to tell him you're looking for him if he comes in later?"

"Yeah," Billy said. "I got to see him tonight."

Pete Pacheco was hardly the ideal customer for any bar. He was the sort who would edge in the back door like a slice of dark shadow and wait for the bartender to notice and bring him a bottle of port wrapped in a piece of newspaper. Then he would pay for it and vanish again until the night policeman might come across him sprawled out asleep against some building in the alley behind Main Street.

But Chuck only smiled. "I'll sure tell him, old buddy. Another draw?"

Billy nodded, drank his second beer slowly, and left.

If Pete came in that night, nobody saw him. But the two of them must have gotten together, because the next thing the town heard about Billy Jenks was that he and Pete Pacheco had gotten caught by the game warden coming down a back road toward town with a big doe they had spotlighted and shot in some rancher's hay meadow. We decided he must of poached deer before and the warden had gotten tipped off. But when we thought about young Jim Mulcahy walking up to the pickup he had stopped and pulling the tarp off the lumped-up, still-warm doe in the truck bed, while Billy Jenks sat in the cab with the old forty-five hidden under his leg, it made us

remember the nickname we had given him and wonder a little....
Especially when we heard that Billy had taken a swing at Jim after the warden had brought them into town.

Of course Billy and Pete were found guilty of killing the doe out of season, of hunting at night with an illegal weapon, of hunting big game without a license, and, in Billy's case, of resisting arrest. The fine of two-hundred-and-fifty dollars seemed a little stiff to some people around town who never had adjusted to the idea of hunting regulations. As for the shoestring ranchers, unemployed sheepherders, and crippled-up bronc riders who squatted in the October sun on the tobacco-stained steps of Stillson's Sporting Goods, they thought mostly that a man had a right to kill himself some meat and one way was about as good as another.

"It's getting so a man can't turn around without getting himself arrested," one of them said, licking together the brown cigarette paper filled with Duke's Mixture.

A rancher nodded, his eyes squinted up against the sun and dust a passing pickup raised from the unpaved street. "That kid of a warden. Been to college a couple of years and thinks he's got the world by the balls. If they put poachers in jail around here, there wouldn't be nobody left to tend store on Indian payday."

"Hell, there wouldn't be no Indians left either!"

There was laughter, and a match flared in the cup of a calloused hand. "I wouldn't of wanted to diddle around looking in Billy's truck the way that warden done. I guess Billy's old man would of given Mulcahy a worse time of it, like he did Pink Rademacher. A man's got some rights left... even if he's a kid who hasn't got a pot to piss in."

With the benefit of hindsight, a person would have to say that most of us sided with Billy to one extent or another. We had felt the Depression, and if there hadn't been breadlines and stock-market suicides in that part of Wyoming, there had been unemployment, some relief checks, and a CCC camp up in the mountains above town with a good deal of joking about what the initials stood for. Besides, the town had almost always been poor, except for a few large ranchers like the Rademachers, some businessmen and bankers, and a couple of Texans who had gotten leases on good structures near the Happy Judgment oil seeps a few miles to the east, where two liquored-up mountain men had been bushwhacked by Crow Indians back in the 1830s. Most of us knew what it was to go hungry at times, to dig postholes in the rocky ground out in the sagebrush for a dollar a day, and to poach a fat doe before the game got all stirred up in the legal hunting season. Billy Jenks was one of us.

"Just a little wild still. . . . Hell's bells, the kid's never had a chance with the kind of mother he had and his old man being railroaded into jail for protecting his family. Some of us got into a lot worse trouble when we were Billy's age."

And if the newcomers in town didn't reason it out that way, at least they were impressed with the stories they heard about Jack Jenks and his boy.

For a while, though, it looked like Billy had gotten tired of giving us made-to-order topics for conversation. His truck didn't appear on Main Street in the evenings, and after a while someone reported seeing him working the gas pump at McClintock's place out on the Sweetwater. That showed us he had more ambition than we had given him credit for. Silas McClintock was getting along into his seventies, a long-nosed old Scotchman with white hair matted down over his head like fresh-clipped wool. He presided over a few shelves of fly-specked groceries and candy, some greasy cases of motor oil, a pile of secondhand tires, and a bar built out to one side of the station with an interior decorated with buffalo skulls, brewery calendars, and a huge print of "Custer's Last Stand."

Every now and then during the next winter, someone from town would stop at McClintock's to have a beer or cup of coffee. There wasn't much for miles in either direction but a cold wind blowing snow across the highway. So you hated to pass the place by, even if old McClintock seemed a little crazy there among those bleached-out, wind-polished skulls, his swollen grey eyes pinning you to your wooden stool at the bar just below the entangled Sioux and Seventh-Cavalry troopers while his burred voice struck at your ears with stories where past and present were mixed in the confusion of his memories.... Until you left with the feeling that maybe he had known Cattle Kate and hidden Butch Cassidy under some ewe pelts in his sheep wagon when the posse was hunting him after the Tipton train holdup.

"Oh, that Cassidy was a fine young man," he would say. "He only stole from the thieving railroads, you know, and who's to say it's a crime taking ill-gotten gains.... The rich ones in the world take everything they can and call it business, but the poor devil of a man who stands in their way is called an outlaw.... A good woman like Kate. It was a cruel piece of work hanging her...."

And Billy Jenks would be there, chewing on a matchstick and leaning against the doorway. You couldn't see anything in his face—someone said it was just like looking at the wrong end of a shotgun—but you had the feeling everything the old man said was soaking in. When you left the bar to climb back into your car, you might see Billy sitting on the bench in the station and reading from a stack of yellowing Western pulp magazines, though people said he should of gotten enough of that listening to old McClintock. Anyway, nobody was surprised when the driver of the station-wagon bus that made the run back and forth to Rawlins saw Billy out behind McClintock's practicing a fast draw with what could only have been Jack Jenks' forty-five. The boy was a queer one, there wasn't any doubt about that, but we figured he would turn out all right eventually, like the rest of us had.

So it came as something of a surprise when the Rademachers began to complain that their cowboys had found a dead cow or maybe a good range bull out in the sagebrush with a bullet in its head. It wasn't a question of rustling, because whoever did it never touched the meat. Pink Rademacher got the brand inspector out from town, and when the number of cattle killed reached twenty-five, the Stock Growers' Association sent their special investigator—"They'll have Tom Horn's ghost out there on the case next," someone said in the barber shop—and after a while they arrested Billy Jenks.

They didn't find his forty-five. But there were tracks that pretty well matched up with the tires on his pickup, and the Rademachers' foreman had seen him driving out one evening near where several RH cows were found shot the next day.

Billy wouldn't hire a lawyer, and when Rife Cutberth, the county attorney, got him on the witness stand, Billy didn't help himself any.

"Yeah, I done it," he said sullenly.

"Then you admit deliberately shooting over thirty head of cattle belonging to Mr. Pink Rademacher and his family?"

"I said I done it."

"Would you tell the court why, Billy?" Rife asked him.

Billy's mouth grew tight and he stared out at where Pink Rademacher sat with his wife in the courtroom. For once Billy's face and slitted eyes seemed to show his feelings well enough, and Pink, who was smiling at first, began to rub his bad arm, and his face grew flushed clear up into the thin reddish hair receding back on his freckled forehead. His wife, who was very neat and wore black-framed glasses, looked at Billy and then back at her husband . . . and then just gazed down uneasily at her hands twisting and untwisting a handkerchief in her lap.

"Why, Billy?" Rife asked again.

"You ask *him*," Billy Jenks said softly. "I said I done it, so you can ask him to tell you why."

Of course Rife didn't ask Pink Rademacher anything, but the people who were there in the courtroom said that was the high point of the trial. Billy was convicted the same day, and it was still early in the summer when a deputy sheriff drove him down to Rawlins to begin his sentence and maybe learn how to handtool the leather women's handbags that the penitentiary inmates were famous for making.

For a while there was quite a bit of talk about Billy Jenks and the trial, but when he wasn't around any more the interest died down. We had already pretty much decided that Billy deserved what he got. On the other hand, we still remembered about Pink

Rademacher and Billy's mother and figured the loss of several-thousand-dollars' worth of RH cattle probably evened things out. If we didn't actually feel sorry for Billy, at least we thought we still owed him the benefit of the doubt. And there was something that caught our imagination about his pistoling those cows... and the way he had stared at Pink during the trial and made him uncomfortable before his wife.

But the town had other things on its mind shortly, for the state was hit with a bad blizzard in the winter of 1949. Stock losses were heavy and baled hay had to be dumped out of airplanes to feed starving cattle in places where they aimlessly waded around belly-deep in snow with their eyelids frosted over. It wasn't so bad on most of the Sweetwater outfits, because the wind kept snow blown off the grassy sagebrush flats. But the Rademachers were unlucky and lost a lot of stock in deep drifts out in the far corner of their winter range.

 Pink turned the ranch business over to his two brothers—Old Man Rademacher had died several years before from a stroke while running a bunch of out-of-state hunters off his government-leased grazing land—and he moved into the town house so his wife could begin teaching school again. At the next election Pink ran for County Sheriff. It was a choice between him and an ex-bartender who had survived several scrapes with the law himself, and the county may of wondered whether a Rademacher was the lesser of two evils. Besides, Pink knew the country and could lead search parties after lost hunters and fishermen. It was true that his gun arm was the gimpy one, but in his campaign speeches on the street corners he always said he could probably still do more damage when the chips were down than his opponent who, in Pink's words, "thought shots were poured instead of fired." Pink got elected, and we said it was just as well Billy Jenks was down in Rawlins....

 In the same summer as the election, the fighting started in Korea, and that caused quite a stir. Reservists were called up, the National Guard was activated, and a good many of the younger men got drafted. And then later, just when the war seemed to be settling down to a stand-off, someone discovered uranium ore out north of the Sweetwater and the whole town was out there with Jeeps and Geiger counters, staking claims and digging test holes in the sagebrush for horses to break their legs in. The first excitement over the town's good fortune to be on the verge of atomic-age prosperity had barely quieted down when Billy Jenks got paroled from the penitentiary and drove through Main Street again in his pickup that Silas McClintock had kept blocked up and covered with a dirty tarp out behind his bar.

Billy looked much the same, a little thinner with even more of the color washed out of his face, but he still had his black hat and his old man's boots. We wondered about the six-shooter—nobody wanted to ask about that, though. Maybe it was only our imaginations tricking us, but we thought he looked more sure of himself, as if he had worked out in his own mind what he was going to do now he was back. So we figured he would probably take a job with a haying crew or pump gas at one of the local stations. When he didn't do anything all summer except hang around bars and drive up and down Main Street in the evening with Pete Pacheco, we said Billy was getting adjusted to life on the outside and that it might take a little time.

It was during the Fourth-of-July celebration that we first saw him with the Indian girl. She was an Arapaho from the reservation with a dark little face, large eyes, and a thin nose that curved down her face like the tip of a hay hook. Her name was Violet Running Bull, and she drove into town every Saturday packed into the back seat of her father's red '37 Buick with four or five brothers and sisters and maybe a couple of aunts wrapped in bright shawls and shapeless print dresses. After the sketchy shopping was finished, Violet and the younger children would wait in the car parked out behind the bars while her father hunted up someone to buy a bottle of whiskey, and then they headed back for their one-room cabin on the reservation in the swerving car where the bottle was passed back and forth among the adults, while the kids chewed licorice sticks, probably knowing the black sweetness was about the size of their supper.

Violet Running Bull looked to be about sixteen, which would of made her seven years younger than Billy. Nobody knew how they met. Probably through Pete Pacheco, we said, since he was supposed to have bought a lot of liquor for the Indians before the law changed so they could walk into the bars themselves and get just as drunk as anyone else in town. During the street celebrations that began at the fairgrounds on the Fourth, Billy Jenks, Violet, and Pete Pacheco hung around together on Main Street. Then after the big dance at the American Legion Club was over, the rodeo cowboys had left town, and everybody nursing hangovers said they were glad it was finished for another year, Billy and Violet began driving around by themselves.

On Saturday nights Billy would park his pickup behind the bars to go in for a few beers, and later someone might see the Indian girl hunched up on the high truck seat waiting for him with those large eyes like a deer's shining out from the darkness of her thin face.

Later that summer one of the town's druggists reported seeing Pink Rademacher pass the two of them walking together down the sidewalk in front of the Penney's store, Billy and the girl both wearing Levis and worn-out Western shirts with tight sleeves and a lot of snap fasteners. Billy was in the process of growing a mustache and some long sideburns, but the project hadn't gotten beyond the stage of looking like he hadn't washed his face for a while. Instead of being neatly braided, Violet's long hair hung down stiff and uncombed to below her shoulders, and she looked like she hadn't been eating any more regularly since running around with Billy. As Pink walked by, he and Billy stared at each other the same way they had at the trial, the druggist said, only this time Rademacher stayed cool as ice. Since being elected sheriff, he had taken to wearing beige gabardine pants, matching jacket, and a narrow-brimmed gray Stetson, and you could usually see his engraved silver star carefully pinned to his shirt where it would show when the front of his jacket wasn't zipped up.

When Billy Jenks had got a little ways down the sidewalk, Pink turned and said, "I've been meaning to tell you something, Billy."

Billy stopped and looked back at him without saying anything. "I wanted you to know I don't have any grudge against you," Pink went on. "As far as I'm concerned you and me are starting out with a clean slate. That business about our cattle has been settled, and as long as you stay out of trouble we'll get along just fine."

For a long moment Billy Jenks stood there with his mouth halfway open and then closing hard as his surprise changed to something else that maybe only the Indian girl could read for sure.

Pink was smiling. "That's right. As far as I'm concerned you didn't sneak around at night shooting a man's livestock and getting sent to the pen. I want to be fair to everyone in this county, including you."

It was quite a speech according to the druggist. For some reason Billy took it like a slap in the face. Maybe he didn't like having so much of his life wiped off the slate by a few words from Pink Rademacher. And after all, we reasoned, he did have a reputation of sorts to live up to.

"You like being sheriff?" Billy asked then, without raising his voice.

"I like it well enough," said Pink.

Violet had begun tugging at Billy's arm as though she was trying to move him away, but he wasn't paying any attention. "I thought you might," he said. "It suits you, don't it. Well, as far as I'm concerned nothing is different between you and me except I been locked up in the hoosegow and you been getting yourself the kind of job you always wanted. You save that crap about being fair for somebody who'll vote for you. I've knowed you too long and thought too much about what you done to my old man to change my mind."

Pink shrugged his shoulders as if he wasn't going to try to change Billy's mind. "I can understand how you feel," he said, "but I think you ought to know the sort of man your father was. He never did a single kindness to your mother. She never knew when there would be any money in the house, because he gambled and whored away his pay as quick as he got his hands on it. If you had seen the bruises he left on her once when he came back to the ranch drunk while she was carrying you, you would feel different about him. My family and I tried to help her by letting her earn some money of her own, but your father and the people around here wanted to believe the worse they could about us."

When Billy heard that, his eyes looked as wild as those of a cornered badger. "It ain't true!" he shouted. "You Rademachers lied and stole.... You scared off or bought out anybody who got in your way out there. That's how you got your land and money. I wouldn't believe nothing you said about my old man, because you'd lie about that too."

"It's true enough, Billy," Pink said. "But I can see you won't believe me." He turned and started walking away.

"You damn right I won't," Billy called after him. "You can't make me believe a god-damn lie like that. I know about you and my old man and why he came after you that night." His voice had become shrill and a little hoarse from shouting. "I know a lie when I hear one. My old man gave you that gimpy arm for what you done, and no crazy lie is going to change that either!"

But Pink Rademacher had gone into the pool hall, and Billy Jenks was shouting to an empty space of sidewalk. When he finally walked off with Violet, he looked like a washed-out, skinny replica of his father, the druggist said, as though he had grown up without ever really being a kid or learning how to be a man. We felt sorry for Billy when we heard about what Pink had told him there on the street. But we decided the sheriff had only been trying to straighten him out, and we wondered if the whole thing might end up doing him some good.

The town watched Billy and Violet Running Bull more closely after that. Most of us thought having a girlfriend might settle Billy down and give him something different to think about. He had Indian blood himself on his mother's side, and we didn't see how either of them could be any worse off together than they had been before they met. If they got married, Violet would have her tribal allotment check to help support them, and we were pretty sure Billy would take a job if he had a wife. So we watched them drive around in Billy's pickup and speculated on how it would work out, while the aspens began to turn up in the mountains and the ranchers with grazing permits on the forest began bringing their cattle down and getting ready to ship their steers to Omaha or Sioux City.

It was still the custom to drive cattle through the back streets of town to get them to the pens alongside the railroad siding and station building on the west bank of the river. Just before a shipping day in the fall, the pens would be filled with steers and dry cows, and from Main Street you could hear their excited bawling for hours on end and then the locomotive steaming in with the slat-sided, manure-splattered stock cars rattling to a stop on the siding. October was a good month for the town. Many of the ranchers deferred paying their bills until shipping time, and there were clothes and supplies to be bought before winter set in. Uranium companies were being formed that fall too, and everyone was carried away with a heady intoxication of the sort that a small Western town can get when it thinks a boom bringing money and growth is upon it.

At about nine o'clock on a Thursday morning, with the October sky clear and deep blue as a mountain lake, the bartender from the Buckhorn ran across Main Street to Stillson's Sporting Goods, his long white apron flapping around his legs.

"Where's Pink?" he shouted. "By God, somebody's held up the bank."

The men squatting on the steps of the store were surprisingly calm at first. "Probably he's at the courthouse," someone said. "You sure it ain't some kind of a joke?"

"Joke hell," the bartender said, breathing heavily. "Somebody just went in the Stockgrowers' and found John Hess and his teller all tied up.... I called the courthouse and they said Pink was up here somewhere."

"Maybe Pink's at the café," a man said. "I can go see. Did you hear who done it?"

The Legend of Billy Jenks

"I heard all right," the bartender said. "It was Billy Jenks. You better get hold of Pink and his deputy right away. Somebody's already called the police."

"Hell, old Carl wouldn't be much help with a bank robbery. I suppose Billy's got his old man's gun too. But dammit, I never thought the kid would be dumb enough to stick up a bank in his hometown."

"Was Billy by himself, Art?"

The bartender was beginning to enjoy his sudden importance. "There was two of them, I heard. Now who the hell would want to help Billy hold up the Stockgrowers'?"

There was an exchange of glances.

"Anybody seen Pete Pacheco around?" someone asked.

By then a little crowd had formed, with people looking over toward the bank and then down at the café to see if the sheriff was coming out. And the more we thought and talked about the holdup, the angrier we got. A few of us had money in the Stockgrowers', while others had been planning to start accounts now that the uranium business was opening up. The bank had loaned quite a bit of money on cattle and automobiles, and for most of us the stone-fronted building with the big plate-glass window and antique interior that smelled of old varnish and polished oak had begun to stand for the easier future and security we thought the town deserved after the uncertainties of a depression and two wars.

"You would think the little jailbird could at least of picked a bank in another town," someone said, putting into words what most of us were thinking.

Just then a voice shouted that Pink Rademacher had come out of the café. He seemed to be looking for someone, and then with several men following he started toward us. We quieted down and watched him break into an awkward trot in his cowboy boots, the sheriff's star flashing in the sunlight under his open jacket.

"We heard the news, Sheriff," one of us called as Pink slowed down to a walk and finally stopped by the front window of Stillson's. "Anything we can do to help?"

Pink stood there getting his wind back and staring up at a bridge over the river, where railroad tracks ended the business district. An automobile jolted by on the street, raising dust and ricocheting gravel off the car's underbelly like buckshot. The window display behind the sheriff was made up of a bearskin rug with the small head forming a vicious grimace of curved teeth and angry pink tongue, a couple of scope-sighted magnum hunting rifles with engraved actions and elaborately checkered myrtlewood stocks, and several yellow boxes of cartridges spread across the grizzled fur along with a few hunting knives, brass compasses, and Japanese binoculars.

"Did they get away, Sheriff?" the bartender from the Buckhorn asked.

Before Pink had a chance to answer, the man who had found him in the café spoke up. "Hell no they didn't. Someone saw Billy's truck hit a telephone pole coming out the alley by the tracks. The two of them jumped out and ran for the express office. Ain't that so, Sheriff?"

Pink Rademacher nodded. "That's right," he said.

"What do you want us to do, Sheriff? You can count on us helping with those bank-robbing sons-of-bitches. You just say the word and we'll get rifles and round up Billy Jenks in a hurry."

"I appreciate your offer," Pink said, raising his voice a little, as though he was beginning a speech. "I don't expect to run into anything my deputy and I can't handle with help from the police. If we need you men, I'll send word back here."

Just then the sheriff's car turned onto Main Street, swerving dangerously to pass a truck and stopping with a squeal of brakes in front of the sporting-goods store. Pink jumped in beside his deputy, who gunned the motor so that the car jerked savagely into full momentum before the sheriff could close the door. It left behind a smell of dust and hot rubber. Before the car turned off by the railroad tracks, the town's police chief, old Carl Anderson, drove past headed in the same direction, his face beneath his bus-driver's cap looking grimly determined, as if at sixty-eight and about to retire, the holding up of the bank had been planned as a personal insult to his long years of giving parking tickets and keeping drunk Indians from sleeping on Main Street.

"Go get 'em, Carl!" someone called out, but he must not of heard it or seen any of us. He just drove on toward the tracks, staring through the dusty windshield at whatever he thought was waiting for him at the express office and keeping his speed down under the town's twenty-mile-an-hour limit in a habit he couldn't of broken if he had wanted to.

There wasn't anything to see after that, and for a while we stood around repeating what we knew of the holdup. But when the first shots came—louder than anyone expected and deliberate, like someone was target shooting—we got restless. Several men said they were going home to get rifles or shotguns, and a couple of the regulars around the sporting-goods store went in to talk to Fred Stillson. We watched through the window, and it wasn't long before Fred came up front and reached over the back of his display to take out the two rifles and the boxes of shells that went with them. A half-dozen of us followed the men with the new rifles as they jog-trotted up the sidewalk while trying to push shells into the magazines, which isn't easy to do on the move with a heavy bolt-action .300 Magnum.

The firing had stopped before we left Main Street. We ran through an alley to save some time and finally found a protected spot behind dry-smelling sacks of feed stacked on a warehouse ramp across from the station building. Dust hung in the air over pens by the tracks where cattle had been stirred up by the shooting. Pink Rademacher and his deputy were bent down beside their car, which had been turned sideways in the middle of the street to give them some cover. We noticed that old Carl Anderson had parked the city police car safely beside the warehouse, and pretty soon he came across the ramp in a crouching yet somehow dignified run to join us behind the sacks.

"What's going on?" one of the riflemen asked. "I don't see anybody in the express office."

"They're there all right," Carl said. "None of us has fired yet, but Billy shot at the sheriff's car as it was driving up."

The other man who had gotten a rifle at Stillson's was looking at the office window with his scope sight. "For Christ's sake, why hasn't anybody shot back? Billy isn't going to give himself up because people been polite to him."

Carl looked around at us tiredly. "They've got the express agent in there, boys. Did you think I came running out here making a target of myself so I could tell you good morning?"

Just then several more men from town came up by the warehouse. They had their deer rifles or Long-Tom repeating shotguns and were making a lot of noise shouting questions at the sheriff or old Carl. Finally Pink made some angry gestures that got them quieted down, and then he turned back toward the faded-red, wood-shingled building which housed the freight and express offices.

"Billy!" he called out. "Can you hear me, Billy? It's the sheriff."

There wasn't any answer.

"Listen, Billy," Pink went on. "I have plenty of men out here now. We don't want anybody to get hurt, so we're giving you a chance to give yourself up."

We saw nothing at the open window . . . no movement of the door. The cattle in the shipping pens continued to low and bawl nervously. It was getting hot behind the feed sacks as the sun began to reflect off corrugated sheet metal forming the front wall of the warehouse.

"You hear me, Billy? We want you and whoever's with you to turn yourselves in. What's your answer?"

We had been staring so hard at the express office without seeing anything that we almost missed the glint at one edge of the window sill and a crescent of pale cheek and dark hatbrim sliding away in the same instant with the heavy slap of a forty-five and impact of the bullet hitting the sheriff's car with a sound like that made by an opener puncturing a can of beer, only magnified several times.

So that was the answer Pink got. And looking back on it, most of us would have to say that Billy didn't really have a choice that morning. Maybe we had one, but Billy Jenks had made up his mind a long while back and we hadn't wanted to admit it. . . .

No sooner had the echo of Billy's forty-five died out than somebody by the warehouse let off a load of buckshot that shattered out the glass in the top panes of the open window Billy Jenks had fired from. Bullets from thirty-thirties splintered wood in the side of the building, and then one of the men behind the feed sacks raised up with the .300 Magnum, aiming at the door apparently. He got thrown off-balance by the recoil, and the muzzle blast beat at our ears—as though a hand grenade had exploded among us, a veteran just back from Korea said later. Afterwards nobody could find where that bullet hit, but the man had flinched so bad while jerking the trigger that it could of gone almost anywhere.

Carl Anderson pulled him down before he could chamber another cartridge, and Pink was swearing at the other men beside the warehouse and trying to get them to hold their fire until he told them to shoot. "You damn fools want to kill the agent?" he shouted. "He's in there with them, so you're just as likely to get him as anybody else."

Momentarily the men seemed to be listening to him and the firing stopped. In that sudden silence we heard the high-pitched, thin rasp of Billy Jenks' voice as he called from the building.

"You listen to me, Sheriff. You say you don't want nobody to get hurt. You really mean that?"

"That's right," Pink called back. "Are you ready to give yourself up?"

We thought we heard Billy laughing. "I ain't that dumb. You and this cruddy town got my old man put in jail and me sent to the pen. If you think I'm going back a second time, you got another thing coming."

"You're all wrong, Billy. I told you before about—"

"You lied, Pink," Billy Jenks cut in. "I wouldn't trust you no more that I would those cock-suckers out there with you."

Billy's voice struck shrilly at our ears as we looked angrily at one another. "All I want is for you to let me come out to settle things between us. You let me out.... And when you get away from that car, we'll draw our guns and start shooting."

When we realized what Billy was saying, we all stared over at Pink Rademacher. The deputy was saying something to him... then shaking his head and arguing back. Behind the feed sacks, Carl Anderson began to mutter at nobody in particular. "Crazy kid... thinks he's some kind of Wild-West gunman. Pink knows better than to take him up on it.... He's a sheriff, not one of those Hollywood actors."

But most of us were thinking about Pink's crippled arm and remembering the story we had heard about Billy Jenks practicing his fast draw out behind McClintock's on the Sweetwater. In the kind of mood the town was in now, there was nothing glamorous about a gunfight — or a wet-behind-the-ears little convict shooting at people with an old forty-five. If once we hadn't cared for the Rademachers, we had in the last hour taken a violent dislike to "Billy the Kid" Jenks, who had spit in our faces with a bank holdup and just finished characterizing us in the crudest terms. We didn't want him to have the satisfaction of killing our sheriff too.

And so we didn't like it when Pink called out to Billy that he was going to shoot it out with him in the street. "Don't be a damn fool, Pink!" someone shouted. "The little son-of-a-bitch can't stay holed up forever."

"I'm making the decisions," Pink shouted back. "I want you men to keep quiet and hold your fire." He clumsily shoved his Smith and Wesson into the belt holster with his left hand — like a man performing a difficult piece of sleight of hand — and stepped from behind the car. "All right," he called. "You can come out now, Billy."

We watched the office door washed in autumn sunlight, the whole scene suspended like a bad color slide projected against the warmth of yellow willows along the river, the rounded slopes of dun-tinted hills, and the blue of an empty, morning-tempered sky. Then the door was cut by shadow, and Billy Jenks edged out, blinking in the sudden brightness before pulling his hat down low over his eyes as he walked toward Pink Rademacher.

Probably none of us had any idea what an old-time gun battle would be like performed right before our eyes instead of prettied up in some paperback novel or a movie. What we did see out in the washboarded street in front of the express office wasn't the real thing either, though it came close. The two figures stopped about fifty feet apart, and Billy Jenks drew his awkward-looking Colt. He got off his first shot while Pink was calmly fumbling for the pistol butt in the tight-fitting leather of his spring-clip holster. Before Pink could draw his thirty-eight with that bad arm, Billy had fired twice more—the booming jars of a big-bore handgun that could be heard all up and down Main Street.

We saw Billy's pale face frozen under the black hat with the bull-rider's crease and his arm jerk each time with the gun's recoil. Then the sheriff fired, the sound small and sharp... lost in another boom from Billy Jenks' forty-five. We saw Pink's open jacket jerk like the wind had caught it.... And then the sheriff was sitting on the ground clutching his side, the pistol lying in the dirt by his boots. Jack Jenks' son had fashioned his revenge—at least that was what we thought.

What Billy did next probably cost him his life. With his last two shots he might of killed Pink Rademacher, though judging from his shooting up to that point the odds were against it. He even might of given himself up or run for the river bottom. Instead he half-turned and fired his last two shots at us with what seemed to be a cold sort of anger, the heavy bullets spanging through the sheet-metal wall of the warehouse and leaving echoes ringing in our eardrums. Then Billy started back past the express office, not really running but moving swiftly like a coyote trying to fade into the sagebrush when he first thinks you might of seen him. He called out something we couldn't hear to whoever was inside the building.

By that time the men beside the warehouse and behind the feed sacks on the ramp had recovered from the shock of getting shot at. They had their guns up, the two men with magnum hunting rifles peering through the scopes and using the sacks to steady their aim. When the express office door jerked open, we knew who would be coming out—that had been pretty plain back on Main Street when someone had asked about Pete Pacheco.

Billy's partner ran out to join him—we saw a hatless, dark-haired figure in Levis and a purple shirt that with more time some of us might of said was too slender and running too fast for a wino Mexican. We saw Billy hesitate as the first shots were fired, and then the two of them made for the end of the building. There was more firing from rifles and shotguns loaded with buckshot. Some cattle in the pens were hit and broke down onto their knees or ran bellowing through the herd, exciting the others with their fright and the smell of blood. Then the magnum hunting rifles were fired, and when the shooting had stopped and a few of the men began shouting to one another, two forms lay crumpled like broken grain sacks on the warm ground by the station.

After we got Pink loaded into a car for the ride to the hospital and found the express agent unharmed inside the office, we carried Billy Jenks and the Indian girl over beside the building. We stood around not talking much and were glad when someone finally brought some old blankets to cover them with. Except for the bullet wounds, Billy looked about the same as he always did. Violet had fixed her hair in braids that were wrapped around the top of her head, and all of us saw the cheap gold ring on one thin finger of her left hand.

In a few minutes a rancher drove up and stopped his pickup by the shipping pens. After he walked among the cattle, he came over to where we were standing. "Let me borrow that rifle," he said angrily to one of the armed men. "I've got two dead steers back there and three more gut-shot. I hope to hell the county's willing to pay for them."

"It couldn't be helped," the deputy told him. "You'll get paid for your cattle. You probably had money in the Stockgrowers' when this character held it up, so you ought to be pleased we got him. This is one outlaw that won't cause any more trouble around here."

Old Carl Anderson was frowning at something as he stood holding the sack of bank money the Indian girl had left behind when she ran out of the express office to join her husband. He took off his cap and began wiping the sweat from his forehead.

"So now he's an outlaw," Carl finally said. "If you ask me, Billy wasn't smart enough or mean enough to amount to much of an outlaw."

Pink's deputy didn't bother to disagree. He looked at the rancher and said, "Let's get it over with."

We all watched the two of them walk back to the pens...and listened uneasily to the sound of gunfire when the wounded steers were shot....

An Arapaho policeman drove into town to pick up the slender, blanket-wrapped body of Violet Jenks and return her to the reservation for burial in the church plot. She hadn't had much of a honeymoon, and we were sorry about her getting shot that way...even if she had been helping Billy hold up the bank. We collected some money around town and sent it out to her father, and the whole family came in the next Saturday night. Somebody bought them two fifths of Old Yellowstone, and early the next morning on the way back to the reservation their rattletrap Buick went off the highway, tore through a barbed-wire fence, and rolled, spilling Mrs. Running Bull, one of Violet's aunts, and two or three kids into a hay meadow. Nobody got killed, but when one of the town barbers said that was only because they were all asleep or too drunk to tense up and get hurt, people waiting in the shop didn't laugh.

Pink Rademacher was out of the hospital right away—just a crease in the side was the way we heard it described. The county paid for burying Billy Jenks in the cemetery on the hill, and Silas McClintock had the headstone put up. It's a place some of the tourists like to visit when they come through town on their way to the Park. The bank robbery was written up in newspapers across the country, so tourists sometimes ask a waitress or filling-station attendant about "Billy the Kid" Jenks. When they hear some story about how tough he and his old man were, they'll spend time looking at the inscription on his stone, taking pictures of the grave, and maybe eating a picnic lunch up there. In the summers the town provides a park table and a trash can so visitors will be more comfortable and won't leave so many pop cans and paper napkins scattered all over. To the tourists Billy is a modern fragment of frontier legend—a young outlaw born in the wrong century, but still tough enough to defy a whole town and shoot it out with the sheriff.

To those who knew Billy Jenks, though, he was mostly something else. He was clumsy and not very bright. He was the hand-to-mouth past that most of us knew too well and wanted to forget. He was our Western innocence—our dream of living free from too many laws, spitting in the eye of authority, and being just as good as the next son-of-a-bitch. But we couldn't forgive him for holding up our bank that October morning in 1952. It was then we realized that his hate for Pink Rademacher was only a part of the greater contempt he felt for the whole town—for all of us who had made allowances and excuses for him while we gradually became a part of the present he scorned... and secretly envied his dangerous incorruptibility.

Maybe that's why we never trusted Pink Rademacher's crooked smile and the shake of his head whenever somebody asked him how it felt to face Billy Jenks' forty-five out in the street that morning. Anyway, we voted him out of office at the next election.

Pink could of lied about Jack Jenks mistreating his wife and the way he had only been trying to help her. Like Silas McClintock always maintained; he could of known we wouldn't let Billy kill him and been smart enough to go down when that bullet grazed him.... Or maybe, though we would never admit it to anyone, the county didn't reelect Pink because a lot of us who smiled at the tourists for visiting that grave on the hill had wanted to preserve for ourselves one last piece of the legend of Billy Jenks.

DAY OF THE EAGLE

HEADNOTES FOR "DAY OF THE EAGLE"

I PROBABLY STARTED TO become a writer when my mother, who had graduated from the University of California and worked as a schoolteacher in an Arizona copper-mining town, taught me to read and appreciate books and libraries when I was very young. By the time I finished high school, I was reading authors such as Hemingway and Steinbeck from the adult section of the county library and writing a column and humorous pieces for the school's page in the local paper's Sunday edition. My graduation present from my parents was a portable Royal typewriter, but my beginning studies as a college student ranged from journalism to geology, with considerable work in literature.

After World War II ended, my father retired early from his career as a petroleum engineer. In 1949, he and my mother bought a small ranch at the edge of the Wind River Mountains west of Lander. While working on a geology degree at the University of Wyoming, I began taking English courses in writing and literature. Eventually I completed an M.A. degree in English, with an emphasis in creative writing, and taught freshman English as a graduate assistant.

My writing teacher was a young Iowa-raised poet named Joseph Langland, who had served with the Army in Europe, was already published in good places, and would soon have a first book of poems published. Joe Langland was teaching poetry as well as fiction-writing classes that required studying classic stories by James Joyce, Faulkner, Turgenev, Eudora Welty, D.H. Lawrence, Katherine Anne Porter, Chekhov, and Flannery O'Connor. And as students we kept writing and discussing together with our instructor the weak and flawed stories we somehow wrote. Over two years I became a halfway decent beginning fiction writer, and the literature courses I took, including a Western American Literature class from Dr. Ruth Hudson, helped my writing and ability as a teacher.

Joe Langland raised money for a literary magazine published by the Department of English, *Writing at Wyoming*, with its first issue appearing in 1952. The second issue in the spring of 1953 was sold on campus and at several locations around the state. "Day of the Eagle" was included in that issue along with three other stories of mine. Its setting resembled my family's ranch, and all I was seeing and experiencing there enriched my writing in what is the shortest and seemingly simplest story in this collection. The narration is in third person with almost everything that happens directly connected to the boy, Dale, and his thoughts. The story uses pieces of experiences and descriptions that were familiar to me. But its plot and theme, the meeting with a girl, the loss of the bobcat, and the ending ride down to the ranch house, form the creativity and art of the story.

At the age of twenty-one, I somehow had managed to write my first piece of fiction that was complete and showed some maturity. "Day of the Eagle" still pleases me for that reason and because the images and details add a subtle depth to what is happening to Dale on this particular day. Although the mounted head of a bobcat hangs on the wall behind me, the reading I did while growing up and what I learned about literature and writing at the University of Wyoming were the strongest influences on this story.

DAY OF THE EAGLE

Dale had never seen the sky so blue. It was a light blue and there were no clouds, nothing except the thin white crescent of old moon. Rounded sloping hills lay under the blue. They were colored the gray and green of sage-sprinkled grassland. Above the canyon cut by the river curving through his father's ranch, he could see mountains with a weathered granite peak rising high over the timber.

He rode closely along the fence to look for broken strands of barbed wire or places where staples were missing. It was almost noon. The sorrel mare didn't want to walk-up, but Dale patiently urged her on. He wanted time to hunt in the canyon. Once he and his brother Lonny had shot a big owl there. They had cut off the fiercely hooked claws. When Dale stuck his hand through them and pulled on the feathery leg, the claws tightened and dug into his flesh. It had been a very big owl. But he was fourteen now and didn't want to shoot another one.

He was on a ridge that rimmed the canyon. Far beyond his father's fence, he saw white dots that were a band of sheep. He started his mare down the steep slope made treacherous by loose shale. Her ears were pricked forward and she chose every move carefully.

When Dale got halfway down, the slope gentled and he was out of the rock. He rode along the canyon bottom, gazing intently at buff-white outcrops above. The sun was hot. Sweat rolled into his eyes and made them burn. He took off his straw hat and dragged a sleeve across his forehead. Up in the sandstone a rabbit hopped into a clump of sage and then squatted to watch him. Dale pulled in the mare as he caught the movement, but he didn't take the gun from across the fork of his saddle. The rabbit disappeared into its burrow.

Already the sun looked like it had been dipped in grease. He was thirsty and remembered the taste of cold water from the hand pump at the ranch when he was a little kid. Heat from the mare's sweaty back worked through saddle leather to chafe against the insides of his legs. He could feel the movement of the smooth muscles in her withers. Ahead of him, beyond the base of the canyon wall, he saw the braced corner posts that marked the end of his father's land. The fence was all right. He started to turn the mare back toward the ranch.

Then he saw the impassive cat-face looking at him from the rocks. The ears were tufted with black. A thick wedge of hair stuck out on each side of the head—a triangular brown head with white around the mouth and black stripes beside the nose.

Bobcat. The word began pounding in his head. *Bobcat.* It's a big *bobcat!* He gripped the twenty-two and fell off the mare. Why doesn't it run, he thought. Maybe it won't. Maybe it'll wait for me to get a shot.

Sitting on the ground in front of the horse, he cocked the rifle and lined up the bead of the front sight in the V of the buckhorn. The cat stood up and half-turned to run. A sharp little crack echoed across the canyon—and the bobcat squalled and jumped for the ledge above. Its claws hung on the rock for an instant and then slipped. The brown body disappeared.

Slowly Dale got up and left the mare with reins hanging. As he climbed up among the rocks, his breath came in short gulps. His hands were moist and shaking as he climbed. Heat in the ledge hurt his feet through the thin soles of his old boots. Finally he stood where the bobcat had been. The back of his throat was tight and dry. He looked around frantically. Maybe the cat had only been wounded. Maybe it got away.

"You can't do anything right," he yelled at himself. "You and your damn sorry shooting."

Tears filmed his eyes, and he cursed them too as part of his loss. Then he saw the dark tongue of blood smearing the block of sandstone. He looked down into the space behind the rock. There was the crumpled bobtailed cat. Blood was beginning to dry around the bullet hole behind the shoulder. It was a big female. Dale prodded her with a stick and then pulled her up by a hind leg. He smoothed the fur on the warm body. Then he held the cat up, a hind leg in each hand. She hung from his chest clear down so the paws and nose touched the rock.

"Hey, Dodie," he yelled. "Look here, Dodie!"

The mare raised her head and watched him with her ears pricked forward.

"She's a big one," he hollered. "What do you say, Dodie?"

The mare gazed at him steadily, then shook a fly from her nose and lowered her head to crop the dry grass. There were clouds in the sky now and one drifted into the sun. It was cool for a while and then hot again as the sun came back out. Somewhere in the canyon a magpie was screeching.

He started skinning out the hind legs of the cat with his pocketknife. I'll have her mounted, he thought. I'll have her mounted with her mouth open, like she was cornered. He skinned down the belly. His brother Lonny would be surprised. There had been the owl, but that was different. He felt the curved, pointed teeth. He could see Lonny running up from the barn when he rode into the corral.

"What you got there, Dale?" Lonny would say.

"Just an old bobcat's all," he would say. And then they would admire her together, and Lonny would go with him to the taxidermist in town.

He skinned out the body and front legs, then cut the cat's neck to free the head and hide. It was hard work to cut through the neck bones with his small knife, but he was thinking about the way he would tell Lonny about shooting her.

Suddenly he heard metal ring lightly on rock behind him. He turned and saw a girl on a huge gray horse watching him from the canyon rim. He was surprised for a moment and then felt awkward. He wiped his bloody hands down the legs of his Levi's. His fingers made red streaks.

"Hi," she said.

"Hi," he answered. He looked down at the cat and the bloody knife on the rock.

"I heard you shoot," she said. "I was herding our sheep down there and I thought I'd come up."

"Oh," he said.

"I thought maybe you shot a coyote. One's been killing our sheep. He got two lambs last week."

Dale rolled the cat over thoughtfully with the toe of his boot. "No," he said. "Just a bobcat. A big one can grab off a lamb quick enough, though."

"May I see it?"

"Sure."

She swung down quickly from the big horse. Her saddle was old and had turned black with age. The reins and bridle were pieced together in several places. Frayed edges of a worn blanket stuck out around the saddle skirts. Finally the boy realized that she was watching him as he inspected her outfit. He turned toward her and smiled.

"My dad bought the Morrison place," she said. "I guess he's been over to visit your folks."

The boy nodded. She was a slender girl with dark black hair that was short and tousled by the wind. Her sunburned face was patterned with freckles and there were even freckles on her lips. He noticed that she wore thin jeans, a boy's denim workshirt, and cowboy boots cracking at the seams. She's about my age, the boy thought.

She came toward him and knelt over the bobcat. "He's big, isn't he?"

"He's a she," Dale said.

"Well, she's big then."

"She sure is."

The girl straightened up and stood looking at the bobcat. Dale liked the way wind rippled her short hair so that it moved in waves like a ripe hay meadow. He wondered what he should say to her. He held his hands awkwardly at his sides. The drying blood seemed to burn into them.

"I've got to clean up," he said abruptly. "Would you like to get a drink at the spring?"

"All right," she said. "Then I've got to get back with the sheep."

Dale carried the bobcat's head and skin to his mare and tied the furry bundle behind the saddle. The girl had ridden down and was sitting on her horse waiting for him.

"It's this way," he said.

He mounted and headed the mare on around the canyon. They rode in quiet except for the clang of iron shoes in rock or a low snort from one of the horses. The trail wound out of the canyon into an open swale dotted with white-faced cattle. An old cow stopped eating and raised her head to watch the intruders. She stared for a minute or two and then started chewing again. Now and then a cow or calf let out a loud bawl.

A scarp ran along the far side of the swale. There was a patch of green below the scarp and willows and small cottonwoods around the spring. They rode up to the edge of the trees. The boy got off and tied his mare to a cottonwood. The girl did the same, and from habit they both loosened the cinches on their saddles.

"The spring's over here," Dale said. He led her to a place against the rocks, where the grass was green and spring water came bubbling out and seeped downhill to run into a small reservoir for the cattle.

Dale lay down on the grassy bank and drank cool water flowing out beneath the rock. After the girl was through drinking, he washed his hands and dried them on the grass. They both rolled over and lay on their backs. Through the opening in the trees straight over them, they could see deep-blue sky with a small sickle of the day-moon centered in the patch. A cloud drifted across and then it was blue again. Dale put his hands behind his head and let his body relax. He saw an eagle sweep over the blue patch with a lazy slowness. He felt suspended high up there with the eagle, looking down, far down, at the earth. If only everything would stay like this, he thought. Maybe nothing will change and I'll always feel just this way.

The eagle finally floated out of the opening and it clouded over again. He could begin to feel the dampness on his back. He rolled over and looked at the girl. She was also watching the patch of sky, and he wondered if she had seen the eagle. She was breathing very softly and her hair waved against the curve of freckled cheek. Dale liked the quiet coolness of the grass beneath his back. He closed his eyes and thought about helping his father stack hay and the warm sweetness of freshly cut timothy, brome, and clover as it spilled down from wooden teeth of the stacker. He and his father would push it out with their pitchforks to build up the sides of the stack, working up to their knees in new hay. Then in late afternoon he would slide off the stack with chaff sticking prickly against his back and run down to the river through the meadow that was yet to be cut, and heavy grass would swallow him up clear above the waist. It would clutch at him all the way down to the river, and suddenly he would burst free and tear off his overalls before he dove into clear water that rushed at him in one cold sweep to wash his body as clean as rocks that lay polished bright and smooth in the stream bed....

He opened his eyes. The sky over the trees was a turquoise with a tiny flaw—the eagle swirling slowly out of sight. The girl was sitting with her head resting against her knees. Dale stood slowly and helped her up. They walked through the willows to their horses.

The girl untied her gray gelding, tightened the cinch, and swung into her saddle. Dale carefully adjusted his mare's bridle before looking at the girl. Her eyes were wide and very blue.

"I guess I'll be seeing you," she said.

"Sure," he said quickly. "We live so near and everything."

"Well, goodbye."

She rode off south toward the sheep, her back straight and small as the large horse picked his way through the rocky places. Dale watched the girl disappear. Then he climbed on his mare and began riding back toward the sandstone ridge at the head of the canyon. As the afternoon grew cooler, sunlight softened colors of the rocks where he had hunted that morning and shot the big bobcat tied behind him on the saddle. Far off somewhere a cow was bawling, again and again.

The ride was mostly uphill and slow going in the canyon. Out on top, the mare put her head down and walked fast without any urging from Dale. When they came to a hill overlooking land that formed a long grass-and-sage-covered slope to the ranch buildings in trees along the river, she began to run.

It'll spoil her to let her run toward the ranch, he thought. It's bad for her legs too. But he let her run and the wind lay sharp against his skin. He felt wild and strange, like he was maybe an Indian.

"Eee-yah," he yelled in the wind.

The rifle in its scabbard flopped beneath the stirrup leather and hurt his leg, but he didn't care.

"Eee-yah," he hollered.

And when they were halfway down the slope, Dale realized there was no longer anything behind him on the saddle. Somewhere the saddle strings slipped loose, he thought, and you lost your big bobcat. There was still sunlight. He could smell sage and the sweaty back of the horse.

"Dodie," he shouted. The mare's ears flicked back for an instant and then forward again. "We should go back, Dodie."

But still he let her run. He could see the rippling dark green of hay meadow along the river below, and he thought of the girl's hair and the curve of her cheek. He wouldn't tell Lonny about the hunt. Maybe someday he would tell him about the bobcat, but he knew his brother wouldn't understand about the eagle.

Often the mare had to break her stride for rocks or clumps of sagebrush, yet she kept running down toward the cluster of trees at the bottom of the rounded slope.

"Eee-yah," he yelled.

WINTER DAYS ARE LONG

HEADNOTES FOR "WINTER DAYS ARE LONG"

A STORY OF RESERVATION LIFE in the 1950s, "Winter Days Are Long: Themes Written by Virginia Shield in Freshman English" appeared in *Quarterly West* in 1981. It was nominated for a Pushcart Prize by *Quarterly West* and by Gordon Lish, an editor at Alfred Knopf, and I was listed in *Pushcart Prize VI: Best of the Small Presses 1981–82* as one of the outstanding writers of short fiction published the previous year. The editor of *Quarterly West* wrote that they had "gotten more good comments on your story than any other story in the last two issues." Reactions from those who read or heard me read the story often related to its tragic realism as well as to Virginia Shield's character and first-person narration through her themes written in a college freshman English class.

Our Wyoming ranch was fifteen miles from the Wind River Reservation on a dangerous stretch of curving highway. What I knew of the state and its people as I was becoming a writer included the Shoshones and Arapahos, their reservation, and what I saw, heard, and read of their lives. They became and remained a part of my teaching and writing. As an undergraduate in college, I had taken courses in physical and cultural anthropology, and during a Coe Fellowship in American Studies at Wyoming as a graduate student I took a year-long course on North American Indians. The class in Western American Literature I had taken from Ruth Hudson, and would later teach for many years myself, always included consideration of the role of Native Americans and their own literature. But in my fiction and poetry I've mostly written of their relationships with white people and culture in Wyoming near the reservation.

Virginia Shield's story is told through an age-old form of fiction, which uses letters, diary entries, or a journal, but with an unusual variation of writing in the form of nine themes for a white instructor in a college class. Among the challenges I faced as a writer were to make Virginia's existence, character, and friendship with Michelle Yellowbird come to life and let her story unfold through the kinds of themes that might actually be assigned in a freshman English class. Although it helped that I had taught a great many composition classes, this story did not come from anything specific I remember students writing. But I do recall the ability of some freshmen to take a standard generalized subject and bring it to life with emotion and the right words.

"Winter Days Are Long" almost wrote itself once I began to hear Virginia's voice in my imagination. And it is the only one of my stories that grows out of a poem, "Elegy for an Indian Girl," which I had written and published much earlier. One of the most encouraging reactions to "Winter Days Are Long" came from a friend in Laramie who was a dedicated high-school counselor and experienced author of books for young adults. Margaret Hill's judgment was always helpful to me and many other writers. When I left the manuscript I had asked her to read, we didn't have a chance to discuss it. A few days later, Margaret told me she was moved by the themes and would like to talk with Virginia about her life and writing. Until I explained the themes were fictional, Margaret believed Virginia Shield was a student in one of my classes. I hadn't meant to be misleading, but now I knew the Shoshone girl writing the themes could be as believable a character as I hoped she would be. And as usual what Margaret Hill went on to tell me about "Winter Days Are Long" was wise and valuable.

HEADNOTES FOR "WINTER DAYS ARE LONG"

WINTER DAYS ARE LONG:
THEMES WRITTEN BY VIRGINIA SHIELD IN FRESHMAN ENGLISH

Theme 1: Introducing Myself
I come from the center of Wyoming where I used to live with my family on the reservation. From this you will know if you don't already that I am Indian. My people are called Shoshones. Once they lived in many parts of the West. I have been only to visit Fort Hall in Idaho. I would not like to live there as our home is in Wyoming. You would not believe it perhaps, but I was very good in school. I attended the high school in town. Someday we will have our own high school on the reservation and our teachers will be Indian. I know college will be hard for me and there will be many problems. I expect it to be difficult, so I cannot be surprised. What I have known before coming here has been hard too. Have you ever visited our reservation?

You have told us this time is to introduce ourselves. My name is Virginia Shield. Many of us were given English names or had our names shortened by the government agent when the reservation was young. My age is eighteen and when you know me better perhaps you will become used to my glasses and how I look. In the dorm I live with a girl from Arizona who is Navaho. She is very pretty. I am still lonely here, but I hope to be a good student. Someday I would like to become a teacher.

I know I have not written as much as the others. I must learn to write more quickly. There are many things I must learn. If I knew more the person I am introducing would not be Virginia Shield.

Theme 2: Description of My Home

You wish us to tell you what our homes are like. I find that hard to answer, for my home now is nothing like the home of my parents or that home on the reservation where I grew up. If I were to describe to you my dormitory it would be as a sad place where people come who want to be lost. They feel nothing for it and it is not a home only a building with little rooms. When I look at all the shiny mirrors in the bathroom I see more bright mirrors but not myself. The house we live in since my family moved from the reservation to town is in a row of new houses colored like candy. My father has a job now which gives him a check each month. He operates a loader at the iron-ore mine. He said he moved to town for my sake which is mostly true, but we lived before without the blue checks. You would think I should be happy not living on the reservation any more? Many people would think that. But the place someone calls a real home remains inside you wherever else you go. This will sound more strange I know, but now I might not return to the reservation even if I could. It would be the same. The problem is that I am not the same. We moved to the town almost a year ago and my father is sending me here to study.

I would like to tell you how I think of the place on the reservation where I grew up. It was in a flat yellow meadow where our cattle grazed in summer. The cabin was of logs made white by the weather. It had a good tin roof and several windows. My grandfather had built a corral and shed of poles from the mountains. From our back yard on a summer day you can see the hump of timber where he went to cut them. The mountains have snow almost all year except for July to October. Our place had no water except for the irrigation ditch, but we could collect rain and haul water from Fort Washakie during the winter. I didn't mind and we have a mineral spring on the reservation where we took hot baths when we were tired of the big washtub and heating water on the stove.

I have one brother and a sister. The cabin was crowded until my father built an extra room in back. We had fun there when it was too cold to play outside. I remember how the sun made a bright arrow across the floor each evening. Mostly we played at being grown and leaving the family. Each of us wanted to be something very different. My older brother planned to be a rodeo cowboy and my sister always liked pretending to be a waitress at the Tee-Pee Restaurant and Bar in town. I thought that would be a good job to have too, though I came to know better. The summers were very hot and in the afternoons we would all stop working in the garden or hay fields and lie in the irrigation ditch until our bodies were cool and our skin began to wrinkle and get goose bumps. In the town there is a swimming pool, but it is always crowded and we don't go there. You can see in some ways that I have one home, many homes, and perhaps no home at all.

Theme 3: My Best Friend

I'm happy you thought my last theme was better in its development. Now I am more comfortable about the writing, though I'm afraid of making more mistakes in the paragraphs and as you say the organization. I will try hard to improve with your help. I'm not sure what you mean about my being "less defensive about being a Native American." But I will try to improve the things you told me about.

I didn't need to think a long time to decide on the person I would write about in this theme. Her name is Michelle Yellowbird and she was my best friend. When we started mission school on the reservation she was the first girl I met on the playground. She was part-Arapaho which made her different from the other girls. I remember she wore a red dress and we laughed because my mother had made me wear a red dress also. At the school we had the same teacher and she was white. I think Michelle was more attractive to her because of her light skin and thin face. I thought she was prettier too. But after we had been friends for several years I realized many other things about Michelle that were important. She was never selfish and would share even her clothes with me. Unlike some friends she would never lie and as we grew older I told her things about myself which I could not tell my family, though we were very close.

"I think you are my shadow sister," I told her once.

"Do you believe that?" Michelle answered. "Is that because I follow you everywhere or you think I'm too thin?"

She began spinning across the scrubby grass behind our house. Her arms were stretched out and her shadow revolved and split crazily. I joined her too until we became dizzy and stumbled against the corral. We fell down on the warm earth and looked up through the corral poles at two of my father's horses. They were huge and misshapen as they snorted at us in fright. That made us laugh harder.

"No," I finally said. "It's because I want to be as pretty as you."

She stopped laughing. "I'm happy you think I'm pretty, but don't wish you were me. You must promise me that."

And I did.

Michelle and I made other friends at the mission school. But I think the other girls were sometimes uncomfortable because of her beauty, especially when we entered high school in town. All of us who were Indian stuck together, but boys began looking at her in a different way. Some of them were white. The way they looked at her or the things they said when they passed us in the halls or we walked onto the school bus didn't seem to matter to Michelle.

We had good times together at football games in the fall before bad weather came. My brother was big and an all-district tackle as a senior. We drove back to the reservation together with his friends after the home games. Sometimes we went to movies in town. And in the summers Michelle made long visits at my home to help with the work. We came to town for the Fourth-of-July rodeo and went to the carnival. We rode the Tilt-a-Whirl until our heads spun and we couldn't walk straight. And we met two Arapaho boys who were riding saddle broncs in the rodeo. It was fun being sixteen and enjoying a long summer before our next year at the high school.

Now you know my friend Michelle Yellowbird. I still call her my shadow sister.

Theme 4: A Person I Dislike or Hate

He was white. I could tell you other things without telling you very much more. Would it matter that his hair was long and blonde as a white girl's? That he quit high school to join the Army and they sent him home for reasons none of us knew? Michelle told me he had a job at the meat-packing plant where out-of-state hunters brought their dead elk and deer, and then other jobs washing dishes in cafés and then no job. He was short and square with bad teeth. His name was Lou and his friend's name was Willie Luther, which made us smile when we spoke of them. His friend was tall and hungry looking. His black hair hung over his eyes and he smoked Bull Durham cigarettes which he made with stained fingers. He lived with his parents while waiting to get a job. Michelle had told me about this and said, "He may never work and perhaps the people in town will call him an Indian."

Michelle had met Lou and Willie Luther at the Bakery Shop one Saturday. The Bakery was where kids in town went to see each other. Sometimes we went too when our families came into town. Lou and Willie Luther were too old to be there. One of the white girls told us they usually hung around the Avalon Bar even though Willie was not twenty-one. Michelle had talked often with Willie Luther, but said she didn't like Lou very much. "His eyes are too white," she told me. "They look like the white gumballs in the machine at Safeway." We laughed together and the next Saturday after the movie I went with her to the Bakery. And after a while they were there.

"Hey girls," the one called Lou said. It was December and he wore an old Army jacket that was too big. His clothes didn't match his shiny black boots. They were the kind paratroopers wore and made him taller. Willie Luther had an old blue parka and funny jeans that didn't fit his bones.

Willie drew out a chair with his foot and sat down. Lou went over to the jukebox clinking coins through his fingers. He walked with his hips stuck out and a strange swing to his shoulders. Michelle stared hard at me and giggled. The record was "Your Cheating Heart."

"What are you girls doing?" asked Willie Luther. "You been to that movie?"

"Yes," Michelle said. "Now we're sitting here for a while before going home."

"Is that a fact?" Willie Luther's eyes squinted in the cigarette smoke rising up from his cupped hand.

"It's cold outside," I said. "That's why we wait here for our ride home."

"No shit. Ain't that something, Willie?"

Michelle and I hadn't noticed Lou was back. Now he was just there by the table pretending to pluck a guitar in time with the jukebox. Willie Luther began whistling.

"No need to wait," Lou said. "Willie and me can take you girls home. Did Willie ask you about driving out there with us?"

"He didn't ask us," Michelle said, "but we couldn't go with you."

Lou hooked thick thumbs in his belt. "You mean shouldn't or wouldn't? You're not scared to ride in my old Ford, are you? No reason to be scared. Willie don't bite and we like In-dans. I got some In-dan blood they tell me."

Michelle leaned toward me. "In his eyes," she whispered without smiling. "That's where it is."

I covered my mouth and bent over. That was when Michelle broke out laughing.

"Something wrong with you girls?" Willie asked. "Here we're being nice and you're giving us a hard time."

"You mean *on* don't you," Lou said.

Afterwards I asked Michelle if she had wanted to ride home with Lou and Willie. She shook her head. "You think I'm crazy? They're both ugly and they're white. Do you know what my father would say about my having a boyfriend with white eyes?"

"What would he say?"

She was very pretty when she smiled. "Your father would say the same thing. But nobody needs to worry when Lou is so short and conceited."

And I knew Michelle was interested a little in Lou.

Theme 5: Winter in Wyoming

Winters on the reservation were very bad. Often there was an early snow in October and then many good days. January and February were hard months when snow was packed over the roads and frozen slick. The days never warmed up and you never felt warm even when the sun came out. Your hands cracked and chapped and wouldn't heal. So the chores took twice the time and effort. Even sleeping late left you tired.

For weeks you lived only thinking about warmth. Each day began and ended in grayness. Nothing changed. Wood and coal smoke hung in the air within our house. Every morning we ate silently, each to one's self, and then waited in the cold for the yellow bus. The gray windows would be frosted over so the ride to our school was disconnected from the world. Michelle and I would sit together sleepily, whispering to each other but mostly staring through the front window of the bus. Kenny White Bear liked Michelle and would lean over her seat to try to talk, but she was shy around him and he would talk to me instead. He played basketball on the high-school team and even some of the white girls liked him. He and I were friends, but I knew it was Michelle he liked.

"Let's go to a movie," he said one morning. "There's a good picture coming about the Apaches. I think it's an old one with Burt Lancaster. We could meet at the Bakery on Saturday. I could bring Bill Tallman."

"I don't like Burt Lancaster," Michelle said. "And you're always off in Cody or Thermopolis with the basketball team."

He smiled at me, happy about her saying something to him. "Next Saturday we don't have a game. Shall I talk to Bill?"

Michelle shook her head and said, "I hate Burt Lancaster and those Apache movies. I hate those Indian girls who only carry wood and cook and act brave when the soldiers attack." She turned around to look at him. "And I hate you and Bill Tallman too."

Michelle said nothing about it until we were eating our lunches at school. "You know about those dances. Guys go out to the cars and drink and then step all over you. Somebody always gets into a big fight. Usually it's some big dummy like Kenny who gets beaten up by a bunch of tough kids from town. I meant it when I said I hate him."

This winter Michelle had become different. Sometimes I wondered if we were still good friends, though I would not betray her by asking. I waited a little and let the noise of the lunchroom fill the silence. Then I said, "Is something the matter?"

"No," she told me fiercely. "What might be the matter?"

"I don't know," I told her. "I'm your best friend and your shadow sister."

That made Michelle look up at me and finally even smile. "Yes," she said. "I am and I want you to promise not to forget it." Her fingers clutched my hand and dug in. It hurt.

I promised. "But you must tell me if anything's the matter," I said.

"No," she said. "Nothing is the matter except the winter. I'm tired of the cold and having nothing to do. Sometimes I wake up at night and see my life stretched out ahead of me like the highway coming in from the reservation. I know every hill and curve and what is at the end."

I nodded. "I know that feeling too. But I don't feel that way all the time. It will be different in the spring when we can get out and have good times again."

"Maybe that's true," Michelle said. "I hope so."

"Yes it's true. And you don't really hate Kenny White Bear do you?"

For a moment she looked like the young Michelle whose thin body spun a broken shadow across our yard at home. "I don't hate him," she said quietly. "Soon you'll go off to college and become a teacher. I want you to do that. Promise me you will!"

I was afraid of her eyes. "All right I promise. And what about you?" I asked.

"Me? I'll be here while you're away," she said. "I'll marry someone like Kenny or Bill Tallman and raise a family and come into town on Saturdays. Do you understand now?"

I didn't understand then, but I thought about it all through English, typing, and girls' volleyball. Even on the bus that took us home through the snowy afternoon.

Theme 6: A Descriptive Paragraph

(I don't feel like writing today, but I will do my best. It isn't easy for me to work in class with only a short time to finish. The room is too hot and the other students write so much that I feel afraid and out-of-place. I have felt this way too often before.)

In the town where I went to school there is a bar where Indians always came. I remember sitting in the car watching through the glass front painted with the bar's name and decorated with beer names and liquor posters. I was still small and I remember the faces of those who came out the open door, the jukebox music, and a strange damp and sweet smell if the car's windows were rolled down. Many years later when I was a senior in high school I saw a man stagger from the same bar and fall into the gutter outside. He was a sick man in stained clothes that had the same spoiled smell I remembered. His face had died. I knew that man. He was Michelle's father.

Theme 7: My Social Life

There is not much to do if you live on the reservation. Now I am busy studying and I don't know many people in the dormitory. My Navaho friend knows some girls and once in a while we go to a movie or walk around the town to look in store windows. She sometimes goes out with a boy from Shiprock. I don't have dates, but this doesn't matter to me. In high school I liked going places with Michelle and some other girls. I liked the friends of my brother and we all had good times together. My brother rode in the Indian rodeos in the summers. It was fun to sit on the arena fence with Michelle and some boys to watch the bronc riding and calf roping. Everyone liked the rodeos. And each summer there would be the Sun Dance which was my family's favorite time.

But the winters were different. You could go to the hot springs sometimes. Or if there was no storm you could ride into town on Saturday and shop or sit in your car to watch the people. Michelle and I liked the movies and basketball games, but we hated the cold months. The worst winter was when we were juniors in high school just after we met Lou and Willie Luther.

One day at school Michelle said, "I saw Willie Luther at the Bakery last Saturday."

I had been home sick and couldn't come to town. "I don't like him," I said.

She told me Lou was there too. I watched her face without speaking. She knew I didn't like them both.

"Lou wants me to meet him next Saturday and ride around or do something."

"What did you tell him?" I asked.

"I'm going to talk to him after school tomorrow. Why shouldn't I go out with him if I want to? If I don't like it I won't let him take me anywhere again."

I felt afraid. "I'm your friend so listen to me," I said. "Don't go with him. When you see him tomorrow tell him you don't want to go anywhere with him."

Michelle smiled at me. "That wouldn't be true. I want to do something different and meet older guys."

"He's white," I told her. "Your father would hate you. Why don't you go out with someone like Kenny White Bear. You know he likes you."

"He's still a boy," Michelle said. "And I want to go places he can't take me. What does my father know of what life is like for me?"

I shook my head. "Please don't go. I'll get my brother and one of his friends. We'll go over to Riverton and have fun."

"It wouldn't be fun for me," Michelle said, "and I think I like Lou. He's been in the Army and has a car. He knows how to have a good time."

"Yes," I said. "He's wild and drinks too much."

Michelle shrugged and laughed. "Don't most people?"

I thought about it all that night. On the bus the next morning I told her to have Lou bring Willie Luther on Saturday because I was going with her. The bus was cold and I was still afraid.

There is not much to do if you live on the reservation.

Theme 8: An Incident Which Changed My Life

You are right about my last theme not keeping to the subject you gave us. I will work harder on "unity and coherence." I want to write better, but what I know is sometimes hard to say on paper.

Some things which happen a person understands right away. This was not like that because I was not there. I should have been, but I wasn't. People told me pieces of what happened and I found out more for myself. And some of it only I know because I was Michelle's best friend.

She was found lying in sagebrush by a side road on the reservation. Michelle fought and Lou had beaten her. Then he and Willie Luther had done the things to her and left her by the road. Lou told Michelle he would kill her if she ever said anything. Bill Tallman's father was a member of the tribal police and he was the one who found her. She was not pretty. Bill's father said she wasn't crying but just sat in the front seat of his car as if something was broken deep inside her. He knew some of what had happened and she told him the rest. He drove first to her family's place to talk to them so they wouldn't worry more about her not returning.

It was very late and Bill's father was off-duty, his big revolver in a holster on the seat. He was a good officer who knew Michelle's family well. He left the heater on in his car to make her warm and walked to the house to explain and help them understand what had happened. It would not have been easy or pleasant. I know that because later I was there myself.

I remember how the moon that night looked frozen in the sky. I can imagine her alone in the car, the side window frosted over near her swollen face. The cold, I think, would have been deep in her bones even with the heat on, the revolver heavy and icy against her skin.

Theme 9: Winter Days are Long

My first semester here is almost ended and it is winter again. In my dorm everyone is excited about taking exams and going home for Christmas. My roommate has asked me to go with her to Arizona and it would be a good thing for me to do. But I can't go with her. It would be warmer there she says. I could meet her family and friends. I tell her I must return to my family, which is partly true. They would be disappointed if I didn't come and I need to see the mountains beyond our house in town.

Everyone will ask me if I have learned much here. How can I answer them? Perhaps I will say I'm sure now I will become a teacher. Or tell them my grades are good. Or tell them how difficult some of my courses were. I want my family to be proud for sending me here.

But there are things I won't be able to tell them too. How sometimes in the dorm I take out the beaded-flower moccasins my grandmother made and feel lonely. How empty a letter from my father makes me because I have never been away before. How I sometimes think I could die here and no one would know. How I lie in my bed in the early morning when the dorm is silent and think about my life and imagine some of it over and over.

I remember riding in our car that night to meet Michelle at the Bakery. My sister is happy because we are on the road to town. She laughs and whispers to me. My father is in a good mood and telling stories about the war he fought in. Lights of a car moving in the opposite direction hurt my eyes. A pickup follows close behind us a long time and then moves out to pass. There is a hill ahead and the pickup cuts over in front of us. My father brakes the car quickly, but the tires slip on some ice and we slide and spin across the road into darkness. "No one is hurt," my father says afterwards. "That is the good thing. The car can be repaired." My mother smiles, but I know she doesn't feel well. My sister is laughing because no one is hurt and I can say nothing while my father begins walking toward Harold Eater's ranch to get help. I wonder what Michelle will do when I don't meet her. My chest is tight and aching, but I can do nothing except try to make my mother feel better.

Or I will have trouble sleeping in the soft dormitory bed and begin to think about the way Lou and Willie Luther were let go. They lied and there was no one who saw them with her, though I told the tribal police my story. Then Lou talked about her and Michelle's father heard the bad things. A year passed. One night he waited near Lou's car parked outside a bar and stabbed him—again and again and again. I can feel the steel in my heart. But I can tell no one.

"Do you hate them?" I ask myself. "Do you hate them all?"

Whatever I answer doesn't really help, because I was not with her. That is what I must live with through all the winters still to come. And because I am Virginia Shield I will.

THE PEACH BOY

HEADNOTES FOR "THE PEACH BOY"

THE WRITING I did during the 1950s was mostly short stories. Part of that time, from 1953 when I completed an M.A. in English through 1955, I served in the Army before doing more graduate work at Wyoming and the University of New Mexico. After spending a year at a small Army camp in Japan, I began writing stories based on my experiences there. I also made two trips back to Japan, was married, and later my wife joined me in New Mexico. I sent a story written at the beginning of my teaching assistantship there, "The Peach Boy," to Joe Langland, who was still teaching at the University of Wyoming and helping current and former writing students in their growth and efforts to publish work. He sent the story on to *The Atlantic Monthly* with an endorsement. After several months it was accepted by the editor, Edward Weeks, who called the story perceptive, "Well-observed, and with a muted pathos which is quite touching." My wife, Yoshiko, came running through the rain from our apartment to the English Department and told me the news.

The reactions from my professors ranged from shock to amusement, and from my fellow graduate students came disbelief, uncertainty over their dedication to scholarship, and curiosity about how much money *The Atlantic* paid me for the story. In 1957 that amount was $300. To us it was a great deal of money, which we used to repay my brother, who had loaned me the funds to fly Yoshiko from Japan to Albuquerque. "The Peach Boy" finally appeared in the September 1958 issue of *The Atlantic Monthly*, when I was teaching at the University of Wyoming. Publication of the story also brought inquiries from four publishers about whether I was writing a novel. I wasn't yet but had been writing more loosely related stories about military life in occupied Japan and the lives of Japanese connected with the soldiers. Eventually I began to recognize the potential for a novel in some of the stories. Sections had to be left out or rewritten, and new chapters added.

With Yoshiko's help in understanding Japanese culture and typing several versions of the manuscript, I finished work on the novel. One inquiry I had received when "The Peach Boy" first appeared was from a senior editor at William Morrow, Frances Phillips, who now read the novel manuscript I sent to her. Frances Phillips became my editor and later, after she retired, a friend. All my writing improved through working with editors, listening to comments from other writers or teachers, and revising heavily. William Morrow published *A Fever for Living* in 1961, and it was reprinted by Dell Books along with Victor Gollancz and Panther Books in England. A reviewer for *Library Journal* called the book "certainly one of the best novels about the occupation of Japan." By then I was well started on a Wyoming historical novel about a family ranching along the Sweetwater River, *Honor Thy Father*, which also would be published by Morrow in 1963 and reprinted by HarperCollins in 2004.

Publication of "The Peach Boy" in *The Atlantic Monthly* changed my life as a writer and broadened my experience with fiction through the two novels that followed. I began teaching creative writing as well as courses in American and Western American Literature. But I also continued writing short stories, including six more of the eight stories in this collection. One of the most interesting comments an editor made on my work was that "I think what you do is develop novel characters in your short stories." I would be delighted if I have done that in some of my stories here.

"The Peach Boy" uses contrasting settings, in Japan and Wyoming, and a traditional Japanese folk tale to develop parallels and ironies as the story moves with a returning soldier, Bill Reno, from East to West. One part of its setting and background helps confirm a belief I've discussed with many of my writing students: If what you know is Wyoming, you can write serious fiction about life and people here just as well as you could about anywhere else. But in the 1950s, the appearance of contemporary fiction about Wyoming and the interior West in literary magazines was rare when compared with published writing from the East, South, and West

Coast. Fortunately for writers in our region, that lack of interest and knowledge improved slowly over time, and publication of "The Peach Boy" in *The Atlantic Monthly* encouraged me to continue writing fiction and poetry set in Wyoming.

THE PEACH BOY

The evening before Bill Reno was to return to the States, he changed into civilian clothes and walked out of the barracks just as the sun, disappearing behind a concrete wall on the west end of camp, splashed orange across the company street. After showing his pass to an MP in the guard shack, Reno followed a sidewalk which ran beside the barbwire-topped wall. Cherry trees along the road were in bloom, with their pink flowers thinly outlined on blue sky. He crossed a patch of sidewalk where an old farmer was sweeping up wheat which he had placed over the hot concrete that afternoon to separate seed from the hulls. A few grains of wheat crumbled beneath Reno's feet. As he passed the wall at the end of camp, he could see a perfectly green expanse of young barley waving a little in the slight breeze. Beyond this field, dark-blue mountains appeared as flatirons stuck up into the sunset.

At the edge of town a bus passed him on the dirt road. Dust swirled and drifted across the road, obscuring even the mountains like some dirty eclipse before finally settling. A humped old man pulled a heavy cart around Reno and moved jerkily past him. By the old man's side, a rust-colored dog strained against his harness, which was fastened to one corner of the cart. Kimono-clad women, bent into obtuseness by the weight of babies bundled to their backs, shuffled slowly down the road near a field of mulberry plants, and bicycle riders rang their bells in warning as they pedaled around the women.

The Legend of Billy Jenks

Reno could smell the damp odor of Japan—a mixture of humid earth and excrement. After a year here, he still wasn't used to it. But you're going home tomorrow, he thought. And the Army will become an unpleasant dream, the country a memory of sights and smells. Tomorrow when a truck taking him to the processing center moved under the arched gate of the camp, he would start to forget. The Army's stupidity... lonely nights at camp... the mess officer who sold part of the post's rations on the black market... a harelipped sergeant who yelled obscenities at his platoon... Japanese bands dragging through American dance numbers at the EM Club on Saturday night... picking up cigarette butts around the NCO quarters. Tomorrow he would start to forget about everything.

Reno cut across the yard in front of a Shinto temple where a crumbling stone lion grinned down at him with long fangs. Barelegged children were bouncing a ball against a wooden wall near the temple. They cried shrilly as they fought for possession of each rebound, but paused to stare with intense brown eyes until he was out of sight.

As Reno passed a small fish shop, an old woman was washing in a copper pan by the side of the house. Her face was shriveled up like a piece of dried meat, and she silently watched him with the knife edges of her eyes. Reno could smell the fish and a more pleasant odor of steaming rice. Farther on, a board fence ran into a maze of little wooden shops and stores which seemed to cling to the edge of the dirt street. Reno turned through a gap in the boards and walked past a garden overgrown with shrubs and stunted trees.

Reno stepped out of his shoes before climbing onto a wooden walkway which led to the stairs. As it was mealtime, this part of the house was quiet, but when he started to climb the stairs he could hear wooden clogs and voices of children playing outside on the street. When he reached one end of the upstairs hallway, he pushed open a paper-covered sliding door. He could see Toyako kneeling on the mat floor near a back window of the large room. She was wearing a gray kimono. Her hair was swept up on top of her head, which gave her oval face a look of forced maturity. The room was almost bare except for a short-legged table in its center. Two quart bottles of Japanese beer and some glasses were on the table.

Usually Toyako ran quickly to greet him when he came back from camp, but tonight she watched silently as he slid the door closed behind him. She pointed out a window at the tile roof where two crows had begun to quarrel. One of them had a twisted, crippled wing which flopped behind it like a useless crutch. Its beak gaped open to expose a blue-black tongue. More crows spiraled from trees onto the roof to attack the cripple with raucous croaks and driving wings.

Toyako rose from the floor to watch near the window. "They don't like sick crow," she said, "so they try to kill."

The tangled, squalling mob flapped across the roof with wings drumming against tile, until the injured crow was forced to plummet onto the ground below, where it was followed by the attackers.

Toyako moved away from the window and knelt down by the table. She opened a bottle of beer and filled two glasses. "The crow will die soon," she said. She drank from the glass of beer and then began to laugh softly, almost under her breath, as though crooning to herself. "Crow is a sign that something's going to die, Reno."

Reno swallowed a glass of the warm beer. When he placed his empty glass on the table, a fly landed inside and clung to the sticky surface. He brushed it out with his finger. "No one's going to die, Toyako. Every day you see many crows and no one dies."

"Something dies all the time, Reno. During the war many people died here. Always there were crows." She poured beer carefully into their glasses. "At first I get scared, but after a few times bombs never mattered. I just stood and watched B-29s and bombs falling. Oh, sometimes they were very pretty."

Reno raised his glass and sipped at the beer. Children's voices from the street below sounded urgent and close in the evening quiet. Tomorrow, he thought. Tomorrow you will start to forget about this girl too. They had lived together for six months in this room, yet he didn't understand her: often her thinking seemed as strange as the catlike cast to her heavy-lidded eyes or the songs she liked to sing while cooking his supper. She had helped him hold onto his sanity, but he didn't really need her. He didn't really need anyone. The Army had taught him that.

Toyako began to talk quietly again. "During wartime the planes came in very low, just over the mountains like sea birds. Many bombs fell and everywhere people die. All down this street there is blood, Reno." She sighed softly and then began to laugh. "But now I have lived with American soldier. Don't you think that funny?"

"Many girls live with soldiers," he said. "They like to have money to buy food and good clothes, and a soldier needs a woman." It was as though he were trying to justify it to himself now, rather than to her. "Many girls need money for their families," he said.

"Of course," Toyako said. "Soldiers come to Japan and live with girls. Soon soldiers gone and then more soldiers come to Japan. Then like trains again gone. Many girls wait at station and one train leaves for trip to the States. Soon another train comes and brings more boys."

"Maybe it's like that," Reno said. "Are you going to wait at the station when I leave?"

Toyako just watched his face and did not answer at first. Then she laughed and raised her glass. "*Kanpai*, Reno," she said. "To wonderful journey to the States." She quickly drank her beer.

From outside in front of the house came the sound of drumbeats. Reno stood up and in his bare feet crossed the mat flooring to the window. A small man in an old woolen Army uniform with ragged puttees had begun to march up one side of the street. As he passed under that window, three little girls clattered from nearby houses to follow the drum. When the old man reached the end of the block, almost a dozen children were crowded around his bicycle-drawn cart parked on the sidewalk.

With thin arms moving rapidly, the old man distributed candy sticks from drawers on the cart and clinked copper yen pieces into a wooden box. The children squatted along a wall of the building opposite the cart. They quietly licked their candy sticks while watching the old man set up a frame of picture slides. When the first frame was in place, he began the story. He had fastened his drum on top of the cart behind the frame, and as he explained each picture he would beat the drum in accompaniment.

"He is telling about Momotaro-san, the Peach Boy," Toyako said. "It is a famous story. He is showing them a picture of the poor woodcutter and his wife who lived alone in the mountains."

The old man tapped on the drum and changed slides with his incredibly thin arm.

"Now the old woman is washing clothes in the stream and a large peach is floating down to her," Toyako said. "It is maybe this big, Reno." She indicated the peach's size with her arms that looked pale yellow in the evening light. "When they got the peach home, the old people work very hard to split it open, and a small, cute boy is inside."

Below, in the street, the story man was holding up a small child from his audience to show the size of the Peach Boy. Then the children stared at the wonderful picture of a boy crawling out from a huge peach.

"The parents are very happy now because their new son is healthy and very good. Oh yes, Reno, all the animals and birds like to come around him for he is so gentle."

The old man tapped softly on the drum.

"The Peach Boy grew up to be strong, and one day he heard about a valley where many bad devils were making trouble for the farmers."

The drum began to beat rapidly and the children were shouting in their shrill, strangely thin voices.

"The Peach Boy's mother made him special food and he went to a deep-in-mountain place where the devils live. On the way he met a monkey, a pheasant, and a dog. They want to eat the food the Peach Boy is carrying, so they go with him to fight the devils."

Reno could hear the children clapping their hands at a picture of the Peach Boy and his animal friends.

"When they got to the devils' country, there was much trouble," Toyako said, "but the monkey opened the gate to their house, and the pheasant pecked at their eyes, and the dog bit their feet. Oh, there was very big fight."

The story man was putting one last picture into the frame. He wove his stick in the air before the children as he finished telling the story.

"The Peach Boy won the fight," Toyako said. "All the devils promised to become very kind farmers and they gave the Peach Boy much gold. Last picture shows devils helping him carry gold to his parents' country."

Outside, the story man took down his pictures, tied his drum tightly to his cart, and pedaled the bicycle slowly off down the street. The children watched him disappear and then, shouting excitedly, they ran off to play. Soon the street was quiet again.

Toyako turned away from the window. "Tomorrow you go back to the States. Why do you go back to the States, Reno?" She knelt by the table. "Many soldiers stay here if they have girlfriends." She rocked gently back and forth from the waist up. In the fading light she looked quite small. "Why must you leave our house here?" she asked.

When the ship left Yokohama, Reno was crowded against a railing on the side which lay against the dock. An Army band was playing, and everyone shouted wildly. A small crowd of people had gathered. Two or three Japanese girls were waving to boy friends on the ship and attempting to call out their goodbyes. Soldiers closest to the ship's railing yelled obscenities at them.

A small girl dressed in a blue suit walked slowly out from the railroad station near the dock. She was looking up at the faces of men who lined the railing. She was dressed very carefully, but in her high-heeled shoes she looked like a doll that a child had prepared for a make-believe party.

"Goodbye, Slant-eyes," someone yelled at her. "Somebody else can wear his kimono!"

Reno wondered whose girlfriend she was. She looked a little like Toyako, which made him vaguely unhappy. As she walked along the ship's side, she held her bottom lip between her teeth as she searched the faces of the men on board. Many soldiers waved or called out to her, but her eyes moved through them and past them as she walked along the dock. Tugboats had started to move the ship out toward the bay. The band began to play more loudly. As the ship moved away, the girl stood very quietly and waved once. Reno watched her change from the still figure of a girl into a patch of blue color, and finally into a small dot. At last he could barely see the dock's outline. The girl was no longer real, and the country shrank into a wood-block print.

All afternoon the ship sailed along the coast. When the sun set that evening, Reno could see trees on the steep little mountains turning into purple. The lights in occasional houses seemed tiny lanterns. As it grew darker, small lights appeared on fishing sampans that passed between his ship and the coast. Darkness painted out houses, trees, mountains, until finally only lights of the sampans could be seen.

As Reno stood against the ship's rail, he could barely see white gulls pivoting swiftly as they picked up garbage thrown from the fantail. Their harsh cries were unpleasant. He thought he could hear a softer wail of another bird high over the ship, but soon he heard nothing except the ship creaking in rougher waters away from the coast.

When Reno came home that summer, the whole valley was ripening into greens and yellows. Wearing a white T-shirt, Levis, and a pair of loafers which were ripping out along the seams, he squinted his eyes into slits like a drowsy cat as he walked down the road into late-afternoon sunlight. His shoes scuffed up little puffs of dust from the road, and the dust powdered over his shoes.

On both sides of the road, fields of hay rippled smoothly. Reno broke off a stalk of hay and chewed on it carefully, tasting the slightly sweet juice and feeling the fibers crush between his teeth. As he moved up the road, three sage hens whirred off in heavy-bodied flight from a culvert and sailed across the meadow on set wings. Reno could feel the sun burning on his back and arms; sweat ran down his face to drip onto the T-shirt. A car rattled up the road behind him, passed, and a woman in the front seat turned around to look at him. Two children in back pressed their noses against a rear window and stared at him.

Down in the valley to his right, Reno could see a stream winding in gentle horseshoes through hay meadows. In back of the fields, shadows inched up rounded, sage-dotted hills as the sun began to set. Reno stopped to take off his shoes and remove a piece of rock. His brown Army socks had big holes in their heels made by his loose loafers. He looked at the steep descent of narrower road that cut through sagebrush before spanning an irrigation ditch and dropping sharply through green waves of hay, to wind among the huge cottonwood trees which shaded a whitewashed house.

As Reno walked through the gate and started down toward the house, he heard a dog begin to bark. Now he could see the red barn he had painted one summer, the corral with two horses standing head to tail in one corner, and the set of elk horns fastened to the crosspiece of its high gate. Under his feet the dry dirt of the road was hot. As he crossed the bridge over the irrigation ditch, a cock pheasant scuttled off through the grass.

Reno could see his mother and father standing by the house and looking up toward the road to see why the dog was barking. As he came nearer, the black-and-white dog circled him excitedly but with caution. She would stop for a minute and watch him closely, then jump suddenly to one side and run a short distance away. All the while she kept barking.

Reno was home.

At first the letters from Toyako, incredibly thin in narrow envelopes which opened at the end and were stamped with two delicately etched goldfish, came about once a week. Reno's parents laughingly questioned him at first, but it came to be like the other subjects connected with his two years of service—after a few attempts to discuss frankly his experiences, he realized his parents did not want to know anything unpleasant, or perhaps it was just that there was no common ground for discussion. He soon kept himself from talking to them about the drinking, stupidity, and brutality he had known, or about Toyako. And after a few weeks the letters stopped coming.

One afternoon Reno stood by the kitchen window as his mother began to wash dishes. She seemed much older to him than he had remembered. Fat was creased on her arms, and the features of her face looked as though they had melted slightly since he had been gone. The kitchen smelled unpleasantly of burned grease, but through the open window he could smell grassy meadows.

"Jean called this morning while you and Dad were irrigating," his mother said. She turned her head so she could watch his face.

"That's good," he said. Looking out the window, he could see an undulating surface of oats on the sloping field behind the house. Far below, next to the river, was the large, chicken-wire magpie trap. Two of the black-and-white birds were hopping around inside the trap. Several others were sitting on the top of the wire or in nearby trees. Reno could faintly hear their excited quarreling.

He turned from the window and watched his mother's hands disappear into dirty dishwater. "She called because she hadn't seen you since you got back," she said.

"I wrote her about everything." He felt a sudden panic. What did they all want? "She knows it's all over with us. I wrote her about it."

Down by the river, more magpies were clustering around the trap. Two of them dropped through the slot on top to get at pieces of rotten meat below. Others spiraled to the ground outside the trap. Their croakings became more urgent and frenzied.

"I just wanted to tell you about it," his mother said. "I guess it doesn't matter to you, does it?"

"No, it doesn't matter any more."

"Maybe you'll change your mind after you've had a chance to settle down. The Cullen boy had trouble adjusting after he got out."

He watched intently as magpies in the trap fought over a piece of meat. "Maybe the Cullen boy and I are different. Some people even like the Army. Some people live like that all their lives." He heard her sigh and begin washing the dishes again.

"Anyway, Jean's a nice girl," she said. "You ought at least to stop by and see her."

He walked away from the window. "But I don't want to see her," he said. "I'm not the Cullen boy and I don't want to see her. I just want everyone to leave me alone."

His mother was silent. The room was completely quiet. He wished everything could always be this quiet, but his mother began moving more dishes into the sink.

"I think I'll go in for the mail," he said. "Do you want anything from town?"

"No," she said. "Nothing at all."

Reno drove the three miles into town and parked the pickup on a dusty street near the post office. He walked up the dirty stone steps and entered a stale-smelling building where rows of little boxes were aligned in sterile similarity. As Reno moved to his family's box at the building's far end, his eye caught the recruiting poster which displayed a clean-shaven young man in immaculate khaki holding a rifle at port-arms. Lettered on the poster in red, white, and blue were the words "He's Guarding You."

It seemed to Reno that he could see in the young face the reality existing beneath an illusion of painted paper: the cruelty of frightened authority in the mouth, the ingrown hardness behind the eyes which came from accepting injustice every day, not being able to protest until the bitterness came to be sustaining. When will you forget? he wondered.

That evening Reno went with his father down to the meadow below the house to tend the magpie trap. His father wore leather gloves and carried a large canvas sack. Tiny veins blotched across the bridge of his nose, which curved in a short hook between pinched blue eyes. "Decided yet what you're going to do?" his father asked.

"No," he said. "I've been thinking about it, but I don't know."

In the chicken-wire enclosure, a mass of black-and-white magpies croaked harshly as they fluttered against the wire and sought for escape. His father entered the trap through a door and with gloved hands trapped each protesting bird in turn and pushed it into the sack.

"Some of the boys are going to school," his father said. "The government pays them, I understand. You used to talk some about going to college."

"I don't want anything from the government. They've done plenty for me."

When his father crawled out of the trap, they walked down to the willow-lined creek which twisted in a narrow slit through the meadow. His father dropped the lumpy sack into a deep, clear pool where rocks lay smooth and rounded on sand that glistened like salt beneath the water. A beak would thrust up through the sack, and Reno pushed the sack down with a stick until the thin streams of air bubbles ceased and the sack lay barely moving in the current.

"Lots of people been in the Army," his father said. "You're lucky to be finished with it. Mother and I think you're making too much out of it. Some boys were in Korea."

"That's right," he said. It was the same thing they had told him in the Army. Don't complain, it could be worse. You're lucky you're not in Korea. It doesn't help to fight it. Conform. Conform. Conform. "You're right, Dad."

Reno watched his father empty the shrunken birds into the brush. Then the two of them walked back to the house through ripening oats which rippled like a girl's hair.

After he had cleaned up, Reno left his mother and father sitting in their small living room and drove to town. He drove up the main street and back down before parking in front of the Union Bar. For several minutes he sat watching people walk past on the sidewalk and listening to snatches of conversation. Many people were in town for Saturday night. They moved slowly along the sidewalks, looking for friends and staring into shop windows. Some were tourists who were stopping only for the night. They stared at drably clothed Indians from the nearby reservation and men in from ranches who wore big hats, boots, and Levis with leather labels still sewed on above the back pockets.

Reno finally went into the bar, where cigarette smoke drifted about the laughing, quarreling faces, the brightly labeled bottles, and the glistening taps.

"Hello, buddy," the bartender said as he sat down. "Been a hot day, hasn't it?"

"Yeah, it has, Red," he said. "I'd like a shot, please, with a beer chaser."

"Sure thing, buddy," Red said, sticking a wide-lipped glass under a tap and carefully drawing the beer. He placed the glass on the bar, poured amber into a shot glass, and picked up the coins. "Thank you, buddy," he said. "Been working hard?"

"No," Reno said.

The bartender laughed. "Me neither. I'm allergic to work."

The beer tasted very cold after the warmth of bourbon. At the far end of the room a jukebox began playing country music with sad, twanging lyrics about lost loves, death, and hopeless sorrow.

> All the night, all the day . . . since you've been
> away . . . who's kissing you . . . just drinking and
> thinking . . . alone and I'm blue . . .

Colors shifted on the jukebox and bubbles endlessly drifted across its face. Reno ordered another drink. Vaguely he thought about what he was going to do tomorrow—or the next week. He had been out of the Army for two months.

A waitress coming off shift sat down near the cash register and ordered a beer. When she smiled, Reno noticed that one of her front teeth was missing. She was a washed-out blonde with a puffy bruise smeared under one eye. A knife-faced man sat down by the waitress, and they began to argue loudly above the jukebox's soft moan.

"So go ahead and sleep with him," the man said. "You think I don't know that's what you're thinking."

"Yeah, I suppose you'd like that, wouldn't you?" She twisted up one corner of her mouth as she talked. "Then you could run to that little Indian slut of yours."

"She may be a slut," he said angrily, "but she's more of a wife than you are. You get what I mean? She don't sneak around behind my back and shack up with half the town."

The waitress twisted around on her stool. "You're a hell of a one to talk to me about shacking up. Oh, sure, I'm supposed to pretend I don't know about your Indian chippie." She squinted up her bruised eye until it was almost closed. "You chippie-chasing bastard."

"Go to hell," the man said. Then he turned and strutted out of the bar.

Putting down her beer glass, the waitress rested her chin on the fat palm of one hand. Her bruised eye twitched as she stared across the bar. The jukebox clacked a new record onto its turntable.

Reno watched an Indian and his thin girl in the back room as they shuffled jerkily to the music. The girl tried to keep him from stumbling as they danced. When Reno turned back to the bar, the waitress was sitting on a stool next to him.

"You've got a kind face," she said.

He could see the bruise and, plainly now, a dark hollow left by the missing tooth. "I'm very kind," he said.

"Yes, you've got a kind face," she said, as though he had not spoken. "My husband has an ugly face. Have you ever seen his face?"

Reno nodded and watched their reflections in the mirror behind the bar.

"I don't let him fool me," the waitress said. "He's a chippie chaser." Her voice slid upward. "He's got an Indian chippie over in Pogue's trailer camp. He thought I didn't know about her, but I seen him pick her up one night."

She pushed her face closer to his and narrowed her eyes against the cigarette smoke. "He ain't got a job and he ain't got my money any more," she said, and winked at him knowingly. "Just that chippie's all he's got now. But she'll leave him, too, when his money's gone." She slapped the bar with one pudgy hand. "I'll have fixed him then, and he'll come crawling back."

The waitress stepped off the stool and started to leave. "An Indian chippie," she said, laughing. "But wait till he comes crawling back."

That night as Bill Reno went to bed, he tried to close his mind completely, as though it were a book he no longer cared to read. Lying in the hot closeness of his small room, he could hear the cottonwoods rustling in a slight breeze. Far away a dog was barking harshly against the quiet murmur of the creek below the house. He began to think about the waitress in the bar, the people he had known in the Army, and Toyako. Each face would appear as a memory he couldn't quite grasp, to be replaced by another and yet another, until the whiskey lulled his senses into sleep.

Then he dreamed of Toyako, as he had on the boat coming back and in the separation center, and she whispered, "Reno-san, Reno-san, why you go back to States?" Why. Why? And he called her name, but there was no one beside him—nothing except darkness. His eyes flicked open suddenly and he was awake again in the same room, but the room was shaking now. The walls seemed to be toppling toward him with a slowness, a sort of majestic awfulness that was beautiful. And he began to laugh, quietly at first and then louder and louder until he could no longer control himself.

"Momotaro-san," he laughed. "Wonderful Peach Boy."

He was sweating and the sheets clung damply to his body. He was cold and he stopped laughing. Very carefully he raised himself up and stared toward the window, where the curtains shifted uneasily in the hot air. But there was nothing except curtains rustling against the screen, like the faintly beating wings of a tired bird.

THE MAN WHO KILLED THE SPLIT-TOED WOLF

HEADNOTES FOR "THE MAN WHO KILLED THE SPLIT-TOED WOLF"

THE WESTERN RANGE land where I've lived for most of my life has also been habitat for bobcats, foxes, coyotes, mountain lions, and, historically as well as quite recently, wolves. My father's side of the family included stockmen, ranchers, farmers, hunters, and outdoorsmen of one sort or another. When I was young, one of my relatives was a government trapper, apparently a little disreputable because my parents always discouraged my desire to meet or learn more about him. I saw many coyotes and heard countless stories about them over the years, and I also read a great deal about wolves and the men who observed, hunted, or trapped them. I believe the role of reading in a writer's development and creativity can be almost as important as experience and observation. But for "The Man Who Killed the Split-Toed Wolf" to be written I needed characters, plot, point of view, a voice, and after that a title.

The starting point in my imagination was an old photograph, much like the one in the story, of a winter-clothed trapper standing with two other men behind the body of a huge gray wolf. The trapper became Slade Wilson, and I had to work out how the wolf was killed and what Slade's life became afterwards. It seemed to me the person who might be most fascinated by such questions would be a boy who thought he might like to be a trapper. I decided the boy would be growing up on a ranch in the Wind River country and telling the story about Slade and the wolf as he put the pieces together himself over several years. From my reading I knew the most notorious wolves had names, usually related to where the animals achieved their fame or some identifying characteristic. And so the story eventually became "The Man Who Killed the Split-Toed Wolf."

When I had worked on the story for quite a while, it was about sixteen pages long in typed manuscript. My first collection of poetry, *Learn to Love the Haze*, had come out in 1976, and the publisher had sent a review copy to a new magazine in Colorado called *The*

Salt Cedar. Its editor, who would become quite well-known for his own writing, was Don Snow. In preparing to print the first issue of the magazine, he needed another short story and had learned that I was a novelist who had written about Wyoming with *Honor Thy Father*. What Don Snow wanted was a story of ten to twelve pages or shorter. Someone actually asking me to submit a story was a new and pleasing experience—one that stirred up all my creative energy over the next two weeks.

The only problem was that my split-toed-wolf piece was four pages too long and there wasn't any section I could leave out. I learned a great deal about conciseness and tightening under pressure, as well as how much writing could be improved with each new draft of a manuscript. "The Man Who Killed the Split-Toed Wolf" was accepted and published in the initial issue of *The Salt Cedar* in 1977. Don Snow later moved to Montana and became involved very successfully with other publications, writing, and teaching. But I always was grateful for his interest in my fiction and poetry, as well as for the work he motivated me to do with this story.

HEADNOTES FOR "THE MAN WHO KILLED THE SPLIT-TOED WOLF"

THE MAN WHO KILLED
THE SPLIT-TOED WOLF

Most people knew him as Slade Wilson, but when I was growing up on a small ranch in central Wyoming, he was simply the man who killed the Split-Toed Wolf. That one thing he had done back in 1920 was what everybody remembered and prized—the only thing of much importance that ever happened to Slade Wilson really... during most of his life anyway.

I only met him face-to-face a few times, though after he came in from the Sweetwater River country and tried to make a go of a little ranch up at the head of Squaw Creek in the 1940s, we would see him on the street every Saturday afternoon, when my father and most other ranchers in the county did their business in town. The first time I saw Slade Wilson, he was coming out of some bar, a faded-looking old fellow dressed in a frayed cap, moth-eaten mackinaw, pants bagged out at the knees and too big for him, like they'd been handed down by some man twice his size, and runover boots crusted with muddy manure.

My younger brother Joe and I were crowded up between our folks on the front seat of our pickup, and as we drove past the place where Slade Wilson stood on the sidewalk, my dad said, "There he is, boys. That's the man who killed the Split-Toed Wolf."

My mother shook her head in a gentle, half-puzzled way. "He doesn't look well this winter. I doubt that he's got anyone looking after him since his sister died."

"No," my father said thoughtfully, "I guess he's living by himself again."

Joe and I stared at Slade Wilson, even after our truck had passed him and we had to turn and look out through the rear window. He had been just the kind of man we thought we wanted to be—living out in the open, hunting, being remembered for doing something great. After all, I had heard my dad tell a neighbor once, when he hadn't known I was listening, that "old Slade killed the biggest son-of-a-bitch of a wolf in the whole damn country." Though later, thinking back on it, I wasn't sure whether or not he had been serious.

That evening at the ranch, I remember, Mother talked my dad into offering Slade Wilson a job handling the mare hitched to the overshot stacker we used in putting up hay each summer. Even though haying season was several months away, Joe and I were excited when we heard that Slade had told Dad he'd come to work early in July when we made the first cutting. We figured to get plenty of chances to hear stories about trapping and the old days... and how he managed to end the career of the notorious Split-Toed Wolf. But when we started haying that summer, Joe was handling the work mare at the stack-yard. Slade Wilson hadn't shown up, and when Mother asked Dad to drive up Squaw Creek to see if anything was the matter, my father was gone for over an hour and then drove the pickup straight into the hay fields without stopping by the house. I remember Dad muttering something about a "drunk old bastard," and I knew better than to ask any questions.

So the next day my dad went out to see Charlie Six-Fingers, a Shoshone who had a small place on the reservation and made his living breaking horses for people in town who wanted gentle mounts to ride summers and in the Fourth-of-July parade. It wasn't much of a living back then, when the town was small and money scarce, but Dad always said he didn't think Charlie really cared whether he sold his horses or not—what mattered was training them right, so they wouldn't spook at passing cars or kick when you walked behind them.

Apparently Charlie Six-Fingers' family had always been loners. My dad told me that back in the 1890s the Indian agent on the reservation convinced the chief of the Shoshones that wife-beating was bad and must be stopped. For some reason the idea stuck in the chief's head, and when he found old Six-Fingers, Charlie's grandfather, laying it on his woman with a lodgepole, he gave him a stern lecture. Six-Fingers must of been pretty stubborn himself about giving up the traditional way of dealing with a difficult wife, and when the need arose he again punished her properly. The chief heard about it, put on his headdress, loaded his white-man's rifle, and walked over to Six-Fingers' lodge. Charlie's grandfather was waiting for him there, wearing his tall-crowned hat and with his folded arms holding a trade blanket around his stocky body. The two of them stared at each other, while Six-Fingers' woman sobbed in one corner of the lodge, and then the chief raised his rifle.

According to the story, Six-Fingers just unfolded his blanket so the chief could see what he was aiming at. And when the chief didn't get any explanation or show of fear, he became angry and shot down Charlie's grandfather right in the entrance to his lodge. The missionary on the reservation was supposed to have said that the price of discouraging wife-beating among the Shoshones was only "one buck," a story that made my dad stalk away in anger when a woman told it laughingly in our house one Sunday afternoon.

Anyway, Charlie had visited our place often. He sold Dad a horse for my mother when her foolproof gray mare died one winter, and she felt good about inviting him to stay for meals and giving him Dad's shirts or a winter coat, along with a lot of talk about her closets needing cleaning and my father getting tired of his clothes before they got worn-out. Charlie would always thank her briefly, and then a few days later show up with a pair of beaded moccasins for her or a hackamore he'd braided for Joe.

I liked having Charlie Six-Fingers there during haying that summer. He was only about five-foot-five but liked to work on top of the stack, moving hay around with his pitchfork to build up the sides straight and solid. He'd let me work up there with him, even though I was light for twelve and not really strong enough to do a man's job. He taught me a lot without my knowing it at the time, and I didn't bother him with too much talk. I remember he liked to tease me a little, too, only it was usually to make a point.

Once we were waiting for the buck-rake to bring in more hay, and Charlie pointed toward the creek. "What do you see down there?"

I looked knowing I wouldn't see what he did, but giving it a try anyway. "Some willows along the creek. I see our fence below the lower meadow... a shed beyond that and some sagebrush, I guess."

Charlie's face remained solemn, but the lines at the corners of his eyes tightened in amusement. "Good," he said. "You have good sight. Maybe if you look more, you'll find that hawk hunting a rabbit in brush by the creek."

I took a better look and did find the hawk, flying just above the green willows and turning back as if he'd located something in a brushy draw.

"Pretty soon the rabbit will get afraid and try to run. That hawk will find and kill him, because he'll die without food. If the winter is very bad and the hawk old and can't fly too good, he'll starve or a bobcat or coyote will kill him."

"That would be too bad," I said, without much thought. "But hawks eat people's chickens and the pheasants."

Charlie smiled at me and nodded. "Everything eats something to live—rabbit, hawk, coyote, and a man too. You know?"

When I was older, I realized Charlie Six-Fingers started me thinking about a lot of things I hadn't seen before.

It was a couple of months later that my father and I ran into Slade Wilson in Stillson's Saddlery and Sporting Goods. Dad was looking at rope halters in one corner of the store that always smelled of new leather and neat's-foot oil, when Slade came in and started dickering with Mr. Stillson over some new traps. I was all ears as they argued about spring poles, blind sets, the Blake and Lamb No. 21, the long-spring Victor, and No. ½ Oneida Jump Trap, but it ended with Slade deciding he could get along without buying anything.

"Hell, I got better traps out in my shed," he said in his raspy growl. "The pans may be corrupting away and the springs rusted up, but they'll have to do. I can't afford any of this new gear you're always selling to rich dudes that don't know any better. I always used to order traps from the Hawkins people, and I never got stung. But this stuff you're selling probably wouldn't hold a stray lapdog."

Fred Stillson got his cigar worked into one corner of his mouth, where he could get a better grip on it, and didn't look a bit ruffled. "You may be right, Slade," he said. "I wouldn't want to sell you something you'd never be satisfied with." He caught my father's eye and winked. "You might have another big wolf up there on Squaw Creek, and I wouldn't want you to be blaming me if he busted out of your set."

I happened to be staring at Slade Wilson's face just then, since it was the first chance I had to see him up close. He had waxy skin that showed red-veined patches over his cheeks and the bridge of a narrow nose that was long and slanted-over on one side, as if it had once been badly broken. He had a straggly yellowed gray mustache, and I seem to recall that his teeth were bad, jagged like broken bones, but what sticks most in my mind was the way his eyes looked when Mr. Stillson jobbed him about trapping a big wolf on his place. They were bluish gray with flecks of yellow in the irises, and the whites were bloodshot. At the time, they gave me the feeling that not only was Slade Wilson touchy about his skill as a trapper, but he might be about half-crazy too.

"So you've heard about the son-of-a-bitch," the old man said. "Hell, I figured the word would get around down here where nobody's got nothing to do except stick their noses in what's none of their business. Well, I don't really give a damn anymore, as long as nobody comes up there messing around. I'll catch him sooner or later."

Stillson didn't let on anything was wrong. "I imagine you will get him. Pretty good-sized wolf, is he?"

Slade grinned. "You won't suck me in that way, not a chance. But I'll tell you this—his paw looks like a man's hand with just the fingers cut. Bigger than the other one even I'll tell you." And he began to laugh, ending up in a fit of loose coughing.

I looked at my dad, but he only seemed amused. Then I heard Fred Stillson say, "You mean bigger than the Split-Toed Wolf?"

"You said it, not me. Like I told you, I don't want nobody bothering me up at the place. I can handle whatever comes around, man or beast." He turned and began easing himself toward the door.

"So long, Slade," my father called out. "Take care up there."

"Don't worry none about me," he answered. "No sir, I'm doing just fine and dandy. Hell, I've got everything I need.... I don't even need no traps." He tapped his old cap with one crooked finger, the nails long and dark as horn. "I'm smarter than any damn scut of a big bastard." And the door slid shut solidly behind him.

I went over to the front window and watched Slade Wilson crossing the street to his dented truck. Several cars had to stop to avoid running him down. In the back of his pickup was a large mottled dog that looked like a cross between shepherd and airedale. It just stood there, about the size of a yearling calf only thinner, and waited, though it didn't really pay attention to Slade when he got in the truck and pulled out into the street without looking back to see if the traffic was clear.

"How about that wolf business," Stillson said. "You didn't know we had one up on Squaw Creek still, did you?"

"I guess I didn't," my father said. "At least it must keep the old boy's mind occupied."

"What there is of it," Stillson remarked dryly. "Let's go over to the café and have a cup of coffee."

Later, when we were driving back to the ranch, I couldn't help talking about Slade Wilson and asking questions. Dad didn't seem to mind it, though, and the conversation with Fred Stillson had put him in a good mood.

"That Split-Toed Wolf he killed," I said. "He didn't really get him in a trap, did he?"

"I don't believe he did, son. When I was young, a lot of the cowboys working out on the Sweetwater used to say Slade was prowling around one bad winter and happened to see him. There weren't hardly any wolves left in the country, and he was big and smart.

After killing him, Slade was hired to trap coyotes by the ranchers out there. They used to use poisoned tallow balls or search out coyote dens in the spring and kill all the pups, but Slade was supposed to be expert with his traps, too."

The road wound around through some grass and sagebrush slopes tilted up by the Wind River Mountains. Down on my right I could see the creek that ran through our ranch and the stripped hay meadows, yellowing already now that the nights were turning cold.

"He looks pretty lonely, doesn't he," I said. "Just living with that dog and no family."

My dad nodded. "I'd say so, son. He had a wife once. Some widow he met in Rawlins during the 1930s. He took her out to a run-down cabin near Home on the Range, but it must have been hard on her, with nobody much around to talk to and nothing to do except listen to the wind and wait for Slade to come back from hunting coyotes and running his trap line. When she finally died, Slade moved into town and worked on hay crews in the summers and drank a lot. His brother had the little place on Squaw Creek and Slade inherited it from him. It would never make anyone a living, though."

I'd seen Slade's place, a log house half-buried in a side hill near a falling-down corral made of poles bleached white by years of snow and sun. There was a slab shed with most of the roof missing and several worn-out truck bodies abandoned wherever they'd been parked before their motors gave out for good. His sister had come to live with him for a few years, and then she died.

"What was his wife like?" I asked.

My father shook his head. "Nobody knew much about her. She killed herself one spring on strychnine he kept around to use on carcasses coyotes might eat. People say he sold out right after that. Just had the shirt on his back and the skin of that big wolf. He even sold that soon, they say, to some Eastern tourist to get drinking money."

I couldn't get it out of my mind, and finally I said, "It's too bad."

"About his wife or selling the skin?"

"About Slade," I said.

There was a book someone had written about our part of the state, and my dad had a faded, loose-leafed copy on the shelf over his desk in the living room. Even before meeting Slade Wilson in person, I had often turned through the pages of that book of local history, looking at pictures of bedraggled Indians posed by dumpy reservation buildings, cowboys with ropelike mustaches eating from tin plates by disappointingly commonplace chuck wagons, and the dusty, unfamiliar main street of the town back in the 1890s.

But after seeing Slade Wilson that day at Stillson's, there was one picture I always stared at the longest, puzzling over every detail as if it held something more important than a man in a buffalo-hide coat and fur cap standing with two other men in front of some ranch house. And there, stretched out before the row of booted feet on the snow, lay a huge, heavily furred gray wolf that even in death gave an impression of graceful power, intelligence, and enormous animal courage. Over the years, though, what drew me back to that brownish photograph—with the figures carefully numbered so their names could be listed—was the expression, the cast of Slade Wilson's face.

He was smiling of course.... And there are limits to how much of a man's smile can be seen beneath a heavy mustache. But as I grew older, I began to wonder if a man could smile when he was deathly afraid of something. If so, that was what I finally read into that photograph of Slade Wilson and the Split-Toed Wolf.

But the book didn't tell me anything more, and whenever I asked some of the old-timers in town about the animal and how Wilson had killed him, the answers I got weren't very satisfactory. "Why he shot the hell out of the big bastard one winter!" I was told, or, "He just knowed wolves, son." Everybody knew the wolf's reputation, of course—how he'd slain sheep by the dozens at a time and, according to stories, several hundred head of cattle and horses. The best wolfers from Wyoming, Colorado, Montana, and the Dakotas had tried their hands at luring him into traps. Eventually the coyotes and foxes had been cut back to the point where ground squirrels and prairie dogs became a nuisance, but the big wolf still made his kills all over the central part of the state, leaving behind the slashed, half-eaten carcasses and the long footprints with the two front toes of one forefoot splayed out by a trap he'd worried loose from.

By the time I got into high school, I had about decided I knew as much as I ever would of the story. As for Slade himself, he was supposed to have taken a job trapping coyotes for some big sheep outfit on Powder River, and I was too busy with school and ranch work to worry much about things that had happened thirty years back. One winter I did try running a trap line along the creek and back a ways into the hills, but after I found a big bobcat snarling and spitting with a front foot caught in one of my No. 8 Victor's, I had some second thoughts and took up my traps. A boy raised on a ranch gets used to stillborn calves, horses ripping themselves up in barbwire, and cows infected from retained afterbirth. So maybe I had just grown up a little... or kept something hidden back in my memory that jarred loose when I shot the trapped bobcat just behind one unrelenting yellow eye.

One day Charlie Six-Fingers came out to tell us he'd taken a job with the reservation police. The rest of the family were all in town, so he and I sat together in the kitchen until they returned. I gave him a sack of my dad's Bull Durham and some brown cigarette papers, and while he rolled a smoke I got down that book with the pictures and asked him about the Indians and scenes taken on the reservation. He answered politely enough, holding the cigarette pinched between his thumb and first finger. But when Charlie's eye caught that picture of the men standing above the dead wolf, he ran his hand under the long length of the animal and then sat staring out through the kitchen window at our horses eating hay on a snow-softened meadow.

"That's the Split-Toed Wolf," I told him. "A long time ago he killed a lot of cattle and sheep around here."

"I know," he said. "Most of them killed to keep their stomachs full, but sometimes one just liked to kill. Some man is like that too and kills animals, another man, but not for any reason except he likes to kill. You know?"

I nodded, wondering whether the point of his talk was the wolf, Slade Wilson, or the way his grandfather had been shot. Charlie was silent for so long that I was startled when he finally spoke. "Do you like to eat wolf?"

"No," I said, and then couldn't keep back a smile.

"This man in the picture never liked to eat wolf either."

"His name is Slade Wilson," I offered. Once I said it, I guessed Charlie Six-Fingers must of known for a long time who killed that wolf, or maybe known Wilson himself. If so, he didn't let on. Maybe he was too busy with whatever thoughts or memories the picture had stirred up. I tried to ask some questions that would get him talking, but I didn't have much luck.

His cigarette had burned out, and I offered him the makings again. After finishing the ritual with tobacco and brown paper, he said, "My father broke horses for one of the ranchers out there and told me the story. The man Wilson made scent from the glands and urine of a wolf bitch he trapped near Lost Cabin. He put the scent on his boots when fresh snow was falling and covered himself with white cloth. The rest you know."

I shook my head. "I don't know. How did he do it?"

Before lighting his smoke, Charlie stared for a long while at the match burning down toward his fingers. "How? I think he knew the wolf's habits and followed the trails he used. But the wolf wanted to mate and was tracking Wilson through the snow. His dog smelled the wolf and warned him.... Otherwise, who knows?"

At the time, I thought I understood.

I was away in the service for a couple of years in the early 1950s, and then began working on a degree in range management at the state university. My brother stayed on the ranch and things went pretty well. The town changed. A lot of new people came in to work in uranium or the steel mill up near South Pass. My dad told me Slade Wilson was back, and we liked to joke about whether anybody had caught a big wolf up on Squaw Creek. One winter my father slipped while feeding cattle and broke his hip, and I stayed out a semester to help on the ranch. Charlie Six-Fingers had gotten into an argument with the tribal council and quit the reservation police. He'd moved into town and was filling-in as a deputy with the sheriff's office. He came out to the ranch sometimes to lend a hand when he was off-duty.

One Sunday about dusk, when Charlie was there and we were sitting down to eat, we got a call from the sheriff. After talking to him, Charlie apologized and said a private pilot flying in over Squaw Creek thought he'd seen a fire on Slade Wilson's place. "You go ahead and eat," he said. "I'll drive up to see what's going on."

"That's fine," my dad told him. "You can stop on the way back and get something to eat if you like. I wonder what the old devil's done now?"

"I'll go with you," I said. "Maybe I can help with the fire anyway." I could tell Dad wanted to go, but there wasn't a chance of that.

"I hope the fire department doesn't have trouble getting up there," my mother worried. "You both be careful."

Dad said, "I'll try calling some of the neighbors. Maybe we can get some help with it. There's enough snow so it shouldn't spread much."

I was thinking there couldn't be much to burn on Slade's ranch, but I grabbed a couple of shovels and buckets and got in Charlie's Jeep. He didn't say much on the way, though he seemed calm. Anyway, he was having trouble with the road, which had been badly rutted and then frozen over, with several deep drifts making it almost impassable, even in four-wheel-drive.

At the head of Squaw Creek we could see Slade Wilson's place, and in the moonlight it looked like the flames had burned down into a reddish swatch glowing against the snow.

"I don't think it's the house," I said. "It looks like his shed."

"Maybe you're right." Charlie Six-Fingers skidded the Jeep onto the side road which passed through a loose tangle of barbwire fencing and dropped off toward the ranch. "I don't see any pumper truck yet, but they won't make good time tonight."

We went on down, the headlights sweeping crazily over snow-covered sagebrush and willows by the creek. And then below us in the darkness, flames suddenly appeared in a wavering pattern of orange and red, and I knew it wasn't the shed this time. Charlie shifted the Jeep into second gear and almost went off the road, but the tires held and we careened even faster toward the burning house. It still seemed to take forever. Then we were stopped a not-too-safe distance away with the headlights yellow against the old log walls.

"Slade!" Charlie Six-Fingers called. "We're here to help you, Slade."

There was no answer, only the sound of the flames, and then a dark shape moved off to one side—large and flowing against the snow. The dog, I thought, the one I'd seen waiting in Slade Wilson's truck, but that had been ten years ago and maybe it was a different one, just as large, though, and with the same look of power and indifference.

"I think he could be in there," Charlie was saying. "I better see. Damned old fool. You wait."

I said, "No, don't try it," but he was gone, a shadow in the headlights that dissolved against the smoke and flames. "Slade," I shouted. "God-damn it, Slade, where are you!"

I heard a howl from down by the willows, but nothing else changed except for the roof sagging with flames. I grabbed a shovel from the Jeep and saw headlights glow above me, where the road from town curved around into sight. As I moved toward the house, there was what sounded like a gunshot and a voice laughing or coughing just as part of the roof went in.... And suddenly I felt old and tired, as though knowing so much all at once had made an emptiness that could never be filled. Stopped by the heat and fire, I called out for Charlie Six-Fingers, remembering the old picture of Slade Wilson with the Split-Toed Wolf he'd killed, the one thing he'd ever done that people admired.

THE LAST LONGHORN

HEADNOTES FOR "THE LAST LONGHORN"

IN WRITING MY SECOND NOVEL, *Honor Thy Father*, I read a great deal about the cattle industry's origin, growth, and spread into the open range land of Wyoming. One book that intrigued me was J. Frank Dobie's *The Longhorns* and his treatment of cattle and men involved in the history and culture of early day ranching. I had met Dobie as a student when Ruth Hudson, my Western American Literature professor who knew him well, took me along when they were to have dinner together in Colorado. As both a writer and university teacher concerned with life and literature of the Southwest, Dobie was largely interested in factual rather than fictional treatments of the region. But storytelling was always an unusually strong part of his writing style, and he was much interested in folk tales.

After listening to Dobie himself that evening and then reading *The Longhorns* a few years later, I began to remember long summer evenings when my father would sit outside with my mother and a few friends. As a boy I would listen to him tell stories of growing up and working on the California ranch his much older brother owned when horses were used in raising grain and alfalfa. It was my father's job to harness the horses early each morning and take them out to a day's work in the warming fields. Late in the afternoons, sweaty and tired as the horses he knew by name and nature, he unharnessed them to cool off under live oak trees by the barn. Each evening he waited to feed them in the corral before walking back to the ranch house, where his brother's young wife served supper and he would finally sleep.

After my father finished a story, the sun usually had gone down and the first stars were out. Someone else would begin another story of an earlier time that seemed in the quiet darkness to hold a deeper meaning to my father, mother, and their friends that I didn't yet understand.

"The Last Longhorn" was begun in the mid-1960s when I was trying unsuccessfully to use a tape recorder for some of my writing and recalled how phonograph recordings had once been a way of preserving songs and stories from elderly Westerners. The old-timer who took shape in my imagination was a former Wyoming cowboy whose memories were vivid but unsteady and who had become a familiar figure in a small-town bar. His story told for a visiting college professor with a recorder is about cowboy life he knew as a boy and a Longhorn steer called Blue Hammer that is a recurring part of his recollections. Around that central scene in the bar I created a frame involving the town itself and some of the modern-day ranchers doing business there and talking with each other. The story is narrated in third person but objectively. A reader can see what is happening and hear what the characters are saying without knowing their thoughts or receiving explanations from the author.

When "The Last Longhorn" was finished, I sent it to what was then a new Western-leaning journal edited by John R. Milton, the *South Dakota Review*. In time I received the story back from Milton, along with some warm-hearted talk of sharing ideas about the Western American Literature courses we both taught, his wish for us to be friends, and the harshest rejection of a story I'd ever had. He thought its focus was muddled, the college professor in it an unsuccessful character, and the story's theme nonexistent. Because the novel *Honor Thy Father* had recently won a Western Heritage Award from the National Cowboy Hall of Fame, Milton wondered if I might be one of those writers who after some success would send off their inferior work to smaller journals like the *South Dakota Review*? And also, again, he still hoped we could become friends.

We did and remained friends until his death in 1995. Over the years, John Milton published a number of my poems and a poetry collection, several articles, and the long story included here, "The Legend of Billy Jenks." Along with the success of the *South Dakota Review* and his own writing of poetry and nonfiction, he would become a leading scholar in the study of Western American Literature. As for "The Last Longhorn," it appeared in the first issue of *Sage*, a literary journal published at the University of Wyoming, in 1966. Most of my writing, whether fiction or poetry, has been revised heavily by me and sometimes after considerable criticism or comments, often from editors. But after its rejection by the *South Dakota Review*, this story still seemed to me to work, through storytelling by an old cowhand, in its consideration of a continually changing West, some of its inhabitants of the 1950s, and the contrasts between myth and reality. But I could be wrong.

THE LAST LONGHORN

The town was in that late-summer idleness between Labor Day and the real beginning of fall. No longer did tourist cars—with children peering out over white arms resting in the rolled-down windows—speed all day long through the main street. No longer were Arapaho Indian dancers hired by the Chamber of Commerce to perform the wolf dance in the evenings and lure travelers into spending the night at local motels. Once more the Wyoming nights were becoming cold, and the sky often was cloudy, as if it might rain or snow. But the warm days continued, and the local ranchers began trucking their cattle into the stockyard for fall shipment.

A few years earlier they had stopped trailing cattle through town on horseback, after a hump-backed little steer had scrambled up onto the sidewalk and butted his reflection in the plate-glass front of the Stockgrowers' State Bank. The townspeople had agreed long before that it was time to stop the trailing; cow manure on the street made the town appear crude and backward.

When the stranger drove up before the sporting-goods store, men squatting on their boot heels by the building stopped smoking, or looking up at the sky, or commenting on the cattle markets in Omaha and Sioux City. Because it was a Saturday, they all wore their town hats of woven fiber, tailored Western shirts, and Levis with big hand-tooled belts. They waited patiently, watching the man open the door of his car and step onto the street with his small black oxfords gleaming like polished horn in the sun.

The ranchers looked at the blue pin-striped suit cut in the style of the forties, the dark necktie that hung loosely from a starched collar, and the man's bare, balding head edged by gray sideburns. They waited while the man slipped coins into one of the new parking meters, completely absorbed in his task, and then faced them. His eyes appeared penetrating but gentle behind metal-framed glasses. The men guessed to themselves whether he was a banker or a well-to-do minister.

"Gentlemen," the man said.

"Morning," one of the ranchers said, shifting his position.

"I drove over from the University yesterday," the man said. "My name is Franklin. I teach literature there."

The men nodded, as if this explained everything. "The boy never took that," one of them said, "but he graduated last year. Guess you wouldn't have known him, though."

"Probably not," the professor said. "You see, my special interest is in the literature of the West. That's why I came over here. I have an appointment with Jason Ikard."

"Old Jake," someone said, laughing. "You mean Old Jake."

"I didn't know his nickname," Franklin said. "In any case, he wasn't at his room this morning, and a woman at the apartments told me he might be in town."

"Crazy Sally.... Did she tell you he was in town all day, every day, Mr. Franklin?"

"No, she wasn't really too clear about it."

"Crazy Sal's never clear after seven o'clock in the morning. Not if she's got any money for wine."

Someone else said, "Ought to have been able to tell him where to find Old Jake, though—wine or no wine."

"Just go down the street to that bar," another of the men told Franklin. "Not ten yet, but that's where Old Jake'll be. He and a few hungover Indians are the early-morning clientele."

They smiled to themselves as the man thanked them, looked uncertainly toward the Buckhorn Bar, and glanced into the back seat of his car. "I wonder," he said finally. "I wonder if one of you would mind helping me unload my tape recorder. It's quite heavy and I don't want to jolt it."

The youngest of the ranchers grinned and took the heavy case that looked like a piece of expensive luggage. "Might as well carry it down," he said. "I'm going that ways anyhow."

The two of them walked together toward the bar, while the little group continued to sit thoughtfully against the building.

"Going to be hot again."

"Rain across the divide yesterday, I heard."

"That's what somebody was telling me...."

"Might go down to take a look," someone finally said.

They all stirred. "Wouldn't hurt, would it."

"Can't you just see him talking with Crazy Sally?"

"Or Old Jake." The men were laughing as they stood up. "What the hell are they going to talk about?"

They all went down together, ordered beer, and stood with the young rancher at the bar. The man Franklin was seated in a booth across from Old Jake with his tape recorder opened on the table top. In a back booth near the pinball machine, Albert Killstwo was slumped down as if sleeping, but his hand still clutched a half-filled wineglass. Two younger Arapahos, their denim shirts completely unbuttoned and long hair falling down around their faces, swayed back and forth as they played pinball and swore at the machine.

The smoky walls of the bar were decorated with prints of Western life by Charlie Russell and Remington. Above the bar's mirror was a moth-eaten elk head that stared out at the booths with cracking glass eyes.

Old Jake still looked tall; he sat perfectly erect in the booth as if it were a long-stirruped saddle. His Pendleton pants were worn thin and had leather patches on the knees. Over a clean white shirt he wore the vest of an old suit. His large cerulean eyes were filmy and then luminous when his speaking focused his attention on a sliver of vivid memory. His face was shadowed by an uncreased felt hat and a sagging mustache of heavy dun hair.

"You are a real old-timer in this country, aren't you, Mr. Ikard?" Franklin was asking.

Old Jake sipped from his glass of straight whiskey. He was unaware of the tape recorder; it seemed to be an object with no meaning for him. "Oh, I worked some of the big outfits," he said at last. His voice was not steady, but it carried clear across the bar.

"Anyone can tell you that much about me. Top hand. Mr. Gunder out on the Sweetwater used to say nobody had the way I did with any critter—horse, man, or cow. When he sold the ranch he put his arm around my shoulders and said, 'Jason, think more of you than my own snot-nosed sons.' And he did too, but he had to sell the ranch. Broke his heart when he done it.... I had a little mare called Dixie used to follow me around like a dog, and one winter she run into a bob-wire fence and the wolves tore her up right back of the main ranch. And I didn't know about it till the morning. Country was wild then and free. Looked like all grass and animals.... I run the spring roundup for our district years and years. Each man had cutting horses and circle horses. Most always circle horses was just green-broke and would be noon before they stopped being snorty and jumping sideways if they seen a sage chicken or kinking their backs like jack rabbits if you tried to rope off 'em. Wasn't this rodeo stuff, hell no. If you bucked off was a long walk and big hoo-rah from all the boys when you got back to the wagon."

His voice died out then, as if this was all he remembered about being a cowboy. The ranchers at the bar had lost interest now that they saw the stranger was just going to let Old Jake talk. Everyone in town had heard about his cowboy days. The Indians struck the pinball machine, tilting it three successive times, and the bartender cursed them into sullen defiance and sold them more beer.

Franklin saw that the old man's glass was empty. "Would you care for another of those?" he asked.

"Early for me but might do it to be sociable," Old Jake said formally.

The professor motioned awkwardly to the bartender, and when the whiskey glass was placed on the table, the old man cradled it in his hands, which were as scaled and deformed as sagebrush roots. His nails were dark and looked like trimmings from a horse's hoof.

"Did your father live in this country too?" Franklin glanced at the revolving spools of the recording machine and frowned to himself.

"My old man came up the trail with the caddle, and both my brothers had ranches on Sun River in Montana. I was on one of the last trail drives from Ore-gon. Was only a boy and the caddle got tender-footed on the lava rock. We lost ten head on one crossing of the Snake...."

When the old man paused, Franklin leaned forward quickly and said, "I was especially interested in whether you knew any of the famous outlaws, Mr. Ikard. Did you ever meet Butch Cassidy or any of his gang?"

"Seen Cassidy on the streets a few times, but I never come to town much." He seemed to grow disinterested again, and he swallowed half of his whiskey at one time. His hand shook as he placed the glass down.

"I thought you might have known him." Franklin was disappointed. "He's a pet interest of mine. Possibly you heard stories or conjecture?"

"Think I seen him once on the streets," repeated Old Jake. "Maybe somebody just told me about seeing him."

The ranchers had started on their second glasses of beer; they began to argue about which teams would be in the World Series and how much the town would grow when a steel company began to develop iron-ore deposits in the nearby mountains. A few businessmen and shoppers passed by outside, but no one else entered the bar. Flies crawled to the edge of Albert Killstwo's wineglass, but even when he raised his head once he did not see them.

"Do you recall any details of the cattleman-nester war?" asked Franklin hopefully. "You were fourteen or fifteen then, weren't you?"

"Was a young man riding line for Mr. Gunder. Broke his heart when he had to sell the ranch."

But then Old Jake's eyes brightened, and his hand steadied so his glass stopped its faint chatter on the table top. "Remember when just a boy one ringy Longhorn cow come up the trail, and first calf she sprung was blue-backed with head and belly white as snow. Later we called him Blue Hammer. That old cow hid him out when we was gathering the caddle to brand in the spring. Oh, we finally marked him, but he growed long-horned and wild as a wolf. Handsome horns he had—six-foot spread and hard as flint. . . .

"Winter we seen them in the rough country, skylining like two ghosts. But when we gathered the caddle in spring or fall that Blue Hammer and the old cow'd snake away. I growed up helping chase that pair through the sage and into the rock. Finally got 'em into a gather the fall I was eighteen and started for the pens at Rock Creek. Second night out we bedded the caddle down in a little flat. They all laid down but Blue Hammer and the Longhorn cow. They just stared around and kept the whole bunch jumpy as cats. About midnight a man riding night guard lit him a cigarette, and when old Blue Hammer seen the match flare he run off full tilt with the whole herd following."

Old Jake sat stiffer and stared past Franklin and the pinball machine as though the cattle were up and running in the alley behind the bar. The tape-recorder's whir was soft but insistent. Several of the customers in the bar winked at each other and began to listen.

"Seen the other pilgrim caddle give up, but not Blue Hammer," Jake Ikard went on. "Oh, hell no. . . . He headed for rock in the Rattlesnake Range and me behind him in the dark, hearing his hooves crunch that granite he'd run in since borned. Sometimes I'd think I could see them long horns shining off ahead and smell sulphur from them hooves on the rock. I rode the dark on little Dixie. Didn't know where I was but wasn't going to give it up without making a ride of it. Come down off the rock into sagebrush, but I couldn't see further than Dixie's ears. Somewhere I heard sage breaking and I peeled my eyes trying to see the white belly of that old blue-backed devil."

Jake lifted his glass woodenly, and when he put it down he seemed to have forgotten what he had been talking about. Franklin had to glance at the wasting tape which continued to slip away in the silence. The bartender brought a fresh drink for the old man without being asked.

"Did you ever find that Blue Hammer steer?" the young rancher called from the bar.

The old man nodded stiffly. "Was getting to that. I ain't as rattle-headed as I look...."

"Well go ahead then, Mr. Ikard!" said the grinning bartender when Jake remained silent.

"Let a man think some, by damn," Old Jake said without turning his head. "Mr. Gunder always used to say, 'Jason, you and me seen more of the real West than all them fellows talking and writing about it all the time.'"

Franklin was embarrassed, but Jake wasn't watching him any more. "Didn't find him that night," he said hoarsely. "I was lucky to find the boys again without breaking my neck. Never seen a hair of him neither until we got back from taking the other caddle to Rock Creek. For some reason I kept wondering about where Blue Hammer had got to when he give me the slip. So I rode the Rattlesnakes and both sides of 'em for almost a week. Boss didn't know what I was doing, though. I recollect that was before Mr. Gunder's time.

"Anyway I did find the damned steer one afternoon not too far from where I stopped running him. Was down in a little gully where he must of piled up in the dark. I spent about an hour poking around to see what must of happened. Can't tell you why but I did.... Figured it out the old boy slipped when he started into that damn gully running hard, big and slab-sided as he was, and drove one of them three-foot horns into the bank. Lying half-tipped-over that way he couldn't get the pry to free hisself. Oh, he tore up the dirt there a-plenty with his hoofs and trying to twist hisself around enough to loose that long horn, but she held him fast as a bear trap. Would have been an awful ruckus to watch that night and maybe the next day too. But the old bastard died right there fighting and raising hell."

"What a tragic end!" Franklin said instinctively.

Old Jake gave a low snort. "Tragic hell! I seen worse ways to take it, and that was just an outlaw steer would have been butchered soon enough anyways. One time north of the Sweetwater I seen a man..."

His voice stopped abruptly, but this time the whole bar was quiet except for the sound of the tape recorder, which no longer seemed to trouble the professor. When the old man said nothing more, Franklin let out his breath—it was almost a sigh—and absently clicked off the machine. He looked as if he wanted to hear something more. But Old Jake had begun to cough, his eyes screwing tight and then becoming watery after each seizure that rattled his entire frame like March wind in bony cottonwoods. Finally the coughing ended also.

Franklin sensed the finality of the interview, and he snapped shut the tape-recorder's imitation-leather case. "Thank you so much," he said, his voice still lowered unnecessarily. "Perhaps another time we could talk again. I would like to hear what took place in those colorful little towns like Rock Creek when the trail drives ended."

The old man was emptying his glass and said nothing.

"Almost no one is left to talk with about the real cowboy life," Franklin said. "I am trying to preserve some stories of cowboys like you. I thought it might make a book someday." He turned to the customers watching him from the bar. "Often when I finish teaching a class, I look out my office window at all the houses and wish I had seen the country as it once was—all grass as far as one could see and those first Longhorns coming up the trail from Texas."

He stood up and straightened his tie. "I'm not sure I would have been suited for such a harsh life, though. There were real hardships during those terrible winters, and few doctors around if you were sick or injured. And imagine the loneliness.... One can almost understand men like Butch Cassidy becoming outlaws or fighting over cattle and range rights. The accounts I've read are fascinating, but I sometimes wonder how much they tell us about what it actually was like in those days."

Old Jake Ikard said, half to himself, "Never seen him after he sold the ranch." He only nodded when Franklin thanked him. He sat just as erectly as when the professor had entered the bar, but he now seemed a part of the bar's interior like the elk head and the sky-splashed prints where horse, man, and distant cattle were lost in the sage-gray of a naked land.

Franklin picked up his machine and nodded to the Indians and the men at the bar. "I wish I could stay in town longer, but the fall term begins next week." He paused, put down the tape recorder, and began pulling out his billfold. "Here," he told the bartender, placing the ten-dollar bill on the polished bar. "I'd like to buy something for all these gentlemen."

And then he was gone. The men saw him pass the plate-glass front of the bar and hurry toward his car with the machine's weight pulling him off-balance like a drunk.

"Nice fellow," someone remarked.

"Lots of work traveling around talking with people that way."

"Yes sir!"

"Funny thing to spend your life at, though...."

They glanced uneasily at the booth where Jake Ikard now muttered fragments of another recollection as his mustache jerked, while fading eyes under the hat brim rolled up like blue stones in their loose lids.

The bartender had rung up the money on the register, and now he was arranging a row of glasses on top of the bar. He broke the seal on a new fifth and made a ceremony of popping the cork. Whiskey gurgled and splashed lightly in the glasses. Jake, the ranchers, and the Indians had turned toward the pleasant sounds from the bar. Early afternoon sunlight tinted the liquid in glasses to the color of honey.

"Wake up the Chief," the young rancher said, nodding toward the rear of the bar. But Albert Killstwo was sitting up now and smiling with dignity, as though he had just come in for a quick one before lunch.

"He done heard the sound of a free drink!" someone joked.

"Come on, old-timer," the bartender called to the booth where Ikard sat.

Another of the ranchers asked, "Did you save them big horns, Jake?"

The old man got up. For a moment he seemed to be coming up to the bar, and someone even pulled one of the glasses toward him.

"Could we have a look at old Blue Hammer's horns some time, Jake? You must of saved them after all that trouble finding him."

"Hell with you! Left 'em lay where they belonged." Old Jake walked stiffly on through the bar and out the back entrance on the alley. He was really a small man and gaunt in the shoulders like an old horse. They heard the screen door bang shut.

Suddenly the men became jovial again, as if they had been restrained by the old man's presence.

"Reckon he's going to see if that Blue Hammer steer's out back!"

"May be chasing him down the street now, scaring the toor-ists right out of their automobiles."

"Never heard him tell that one before. Blue Hammer!"

All the ranchers except the young one who had helped Franklin began to laugh and add embellishments to the story, until they forgot the way Old Jake had made it all come to life. The bartender got Albert Killstwo and the vacant-eyed younger Indians up to the bar and had a drink himself from Franklin's ten-dollar bill. When the ranchers left, the bar was noisy again with pinball bells and the muttering monologue Albert always used in trying to persuade the bartender to give him credit until the next Indian payday.

Outside, the sun was harsh in fading-blue September sky. The ranchers blinked and pulled their hats down to shade their eyes from the starkness of sand-colored buildings and the highway bisecting them perfectly. They watched the automobile slip away from the curb and follow the highway to the end of town, cross the bridge over the river, and climb up the hill toward the east. The car became a blue smudge on the asphalt, and at the highest part of the hill by the cemetery, the rear windshield seemed to shatter in reflected sunlight as the car vanished.

"Going out to the place?" one of the men asked.

"Might as well. You?"

"Supposed to be a machinery salesman coming out this afternoon."

"You going to get another John Deere?"

"Might."

The ranchers paused in front of the sporting-goods store, as if reluctant to separate and return to the loneliness of their work.

"Where do you suppose the old man is?" the young rancher asked abruptly.

"Still chasing old Blue Hammer, maybe," one of them said, attempting to prolong the joke.

But the young rancher did not smile. "Don't you ever feel you'd like to have seen the country then? Like the professor told about wishing? The way Old Jake knew it."

"Probably the old boy just dreamed it was like that anyways. Everybody knows how he lies when he's got a good drunk going. He didn't even save that set of horns. Bet they'd be something to see—if there really was a steer like that."

"He didn't need to save no horns," the young rancher said angrily, looking back down the street to see if Jake was there.

"Maybe he didn't or maybe he couldn't," one of his friends said, lighting a cigarette. "It ain't worth getting upset about. Why next thing we know you'll be down at the University telling stories to the professor's re-corder just like Old Jake."

Finally the young rancher began to see the humor in this and started to grin a little. "Maybe you're right at that," he said. And by the time the conversation got around to the new iron-ore project, he had stopped looking back for the old man and was talking louder than anyone else.

LEAVE'S END

HEADNOTES FOR "LEAVE'S END"

"LEAVE'S END" is a story set in the Wind River country during the Vietnam War. It first appeared in *Writers' Forum* in 1989 and was reprinted in their anthology *Higher Elevations: Stories from the West*, published in 1993 by Swallow Press/Ohio University Press. Unlike "The Last Longhorn" and many other stories of mine, "Leave's End" kept changing over a long period of time while I was writing it and again after difficulties in finding a publisher for it. I submitted it to about a dozen places ranging from *The Atlantic Monthly* to *Virginia Quarterly Review*. The story received encouraging responses from about half of the editors, was lost for a year and half by one well-known Midwest quarterly which finally found and praised it three years later, had been almost taken by another quarterly after eight months, and was accepted by a magazine called *Fiction* in Boston, which then slowly went out of the business while assuring me they weren't.

Some editors' comments simply said the story was too long, and that that they liked ones that were under 3,000 words. The revisions I went on to make, though, actually lengthened it even more. But by then I didn't think anything I did could make the story more difficult to write and publish than it already seemed to be. Earlier I had submitted to *Writers' Forum* a different story which was rejected, and when the editor, Alexander Blackburn, asked if I had another piece for him to consider, I sent off "Leave's End" and it was accepted. When it was selected for the *Higher Elevations* anthology, one of the editors, C. Kenneth Pellow, wrote in a headnote for the story that "In its final moments, 'Leave's End' puts a twist upon hopefulness in a way that perhaps no other story here does.... Even this, gloomy though it finally becomes, is a story that celebrates life, as evidenced by the appeal to Runner—and to a lesser extent, to Kathy—of the smells of hay, clover, the river, all of nature." He also pointed out the story's use of ironies involving the concepts of "escape" and "entrapment." This undoubtedly is true. But I would hope there is growth and change in John Runner and Kathy which is not only sometimes ironic, but decisive and positive as well as final.

Authors are often advised to write about what they know or, in my view, can find out in one way or another. I had been drafted into the Army in the 1950s with other men about my age from a small town surrounded by ranches, farms, and the reservation. But this was at the end of the Korean War. During the fighting in Vietnam, I was teaching draft-age men who were university students or later, as the years went on, returning veterans of the war who were starting or coming back to school. A number of them were taking creative-writing courses and working on stories or poems related to the war and its impact. Among them was Major Ted Gostas of Cheyenne, who had been a prisoner in North Vietnam for four-and-a-half years and wrote a powerful treatment of military life and the war while completing an English M.A. in 1978.

But "Leave's End" had always been about life on a Wyoming ranch during the Vietnam War when a young soldier is home on leave after basic training. The story uses a third-person point of view which closely follows John Runner's actions, observations, and thoughts. I had been through basic training, knew the country this story has as its setting, worked in hay fields for my own and other ranching families, and admired girls who grew up on the land. But those are only pieces of reality that supported and stirred my imagination into forming characters, actions, scenes, and outcomes that eventually turned "Leave's End" into fiction that hopefully readers will feel and remember.

LEAVE'S END

Through the rolled-down window of his father's old Ford pickup, the world smelled of ripe hay. And when John Runner turned off the highway near the Manderson ranch, meadows below the dirt road spread smoothly down the valley, with the river marked on his left by a line of cottonwoods and willows that leaned over the water like tired arms. The trees appeared pale under early morning light, as if the river was drawing their color into its darker surface. In the nearest field, a crew of Arapahos wearing denim clothing and red or blue baseball caps rode buck-rakes and hydraulic stackers that clawed upward over the tractors when nearing the half-completed haystack. Runner raised one hand in greeting. Amos Spearhunter lived near his father's place on the reservation. His father had died of pneumonia four years ago, after helping Amos and some relatives gather cattle in a blizzard during calving season.

The popping exhaust of Farmalls and John Deeres seemed very close and then faded out as the road curved away from the river. Their sound reminded him of the Army camp in Kansas and machine-gun fire on the infiltration course. He had often heard it while lying awake in the dark barracks, and when his company had gone on field problems at night, preparing for what they knew would probably be combat in Vietnam, the sound became urgent like spring insects.

As the noise of the tractors died in his ears, it seemed to John Runner that his leave had somehow passed without his being aware of it. Although four days remained, he experienced the same feeling as he had early that morning in the small ranch house north of Ethete where he had been born. Suspended between dream and sunlight, he had been certain he was again in the barracks. The last days of his leave had vanished while he slept, and he was listening for the first sound of morning—the spring tightening on a door as the platoon sergeant entered the quarters to snap on the lights. In some ways it was a comfortable feeling to know how each day would start and end. Now when his leave was almost gone, he had begun to realize that he missed the impersonal, rootless life of a soldier....

Ahead of the pickup, Runner could see dun foothills above the ranch where he had been helping Kathy Manderson's father put up hay. The white house, barn, and sheds were down near the river, and in bright sunlight they hurt his eyes. He slowed the Ford as he drove past the patch of wild roses where he had parked the night before, when bringing Kathy home from a Western movie in town, and they had smelled the hay—clean, dry, faintly sweet, and tinged with the rankness of yellow clover. It will all work itself out when I see her, he thought, remembering the soft curve of her cheek against his face as he had watched reflections on the windshield from lights of heavy trucks low-gearing up a steep stretch of highway behind them.

It was the same piece of road on which his older brother, driving back to the reservation after a Fourth-of-July celebration in town, had weaved into a tourist car, killing the driver and his wife. At his trial Delbert claimed he swerved that night to miss loose horses crossing the highway, and had taken off on foot after the accident and hidden for three days because of a head injury. While John Runner was waiting to be drafted, Delbert had begun a long sentence in the Fremont County Jail for drunk driving, hit-and-run, and involuntary manslaughter. Delbert hated ranch work and living on the reservation with his mother, and had often been in trouble. Once he stabbed a liquor-store clerk in town during a fight over a woman they both had been sleeping with. But she had persuaded the man to drop the charges if she would stop seeing

Delbert. The car wreck was different. His brother couldn't pay for a good lawyer—even some townspeople admitted that, and a few of them went out of their way to show they felt no differently toward John. But Kathy's mother made her opinion clear enough. She had come out to the reservation to tell Mrs. Runner that her daughter would never marry a half-breed whose drunken brother was in jail and live like an Indian on tribal payments and government handouts.

In the parked pickup last night, Kathy's freckled face had seemed almost as brown as his own skin. When they were alone together, she had a way of curling up her legs on the seat and lying back against him. She wore a sleeveless blouse with her starched Levis, and he could feel her smooth, work-hardened arm under his palm. For most of her life, she had helped out on her father's ranch and was direct like a boy in her talk and actions, yet quiet and gentle too, so that he never thought of her as a tomboy.

"Why are you thinking so hard?" she asked, her hand resting warm on his thigh. "Is your leave different than you thought it would be?"

His answer was half-true. "I was watching the trucks back there. I'm glad we can't hear them."

"It's always peaceful here at night. Do you remember how we used to stop and talk after basketball games in high school?"

He remembered that, and how good it felt during his senior year, when he made all-conference as a guard, to know Kathy was in the stands watching him play. On the drive to her place, he would park here, where dead rose branches were frozen in the wire fence, and turn up her face until their cool mouths came together and the tension of the game slipped away from him like melting spring snow....

"Twenty more months isn't too long," Kathy had said last night. "I'll get a job and save some money. Your brother doesn't want to stay on your parents' place, and we could live there. Someday we could lease more grazing land and run a bigger herd of cattle, like we used to talk about doing."

'He wasn't sure whether it was her hair he smelled or the hay. "It's almost two years," he said. "That's a long time off. Maybe in two years we won't want to do that."

For a moment her face, touched by moonlight, seemed much older. "We will," she told him. "I know we will. Mother won't be able to stop us from getting married then, and the Army won't keep us apart either."

He started to say he was thinking about staying in the Army, where no one knew or cared that his father had been an Arapaho named Jack Slow Runner who married a white woman, and they tried for twenty-five years to survive on the reservation with two children and not enough land, cattle, or money... that his brother was unable to find a life for himself there or in town, and one drunken night had ended up killing two people. He had watched his father and mother struggle to stay together despite their differences, raise him and Delbert the best they could, even though she and the boys often felt like outsiders. His father had been contented there among his relatives. He owned too many horses and some cattle, followed the peyote way, and tried to get along on tribal allotment checks and a little ranching income. His mother worried about paying for groceries, clothes for the family, repairs on the pickup and tractor when they broke down during haying season or the long winters. Runner could remember her standing at the sink in their log house, gazing out the small window at the snow or grass, as though watching for some change she no longer expected. . . .

But he didn't tell Kathy what was on his mind. He was having difficulty admitting, even to himself, that his feelings about marrying her had been changing while his hands were being hardened by steel weapons during basic training. Later, lying in his bed after taking her home, he had decided she belonged to an earlier time and place he wanted to escape from—that he would have no need for in a few days when he went beneath the guarded gates of another camp for reassignment overseas, carrying all his possessions in the duffel bag on his shoulder. With what it contained and a rifle, helmet, and combat pack, he was equipped to kill enemy soldiers, civilians, rioters—anyone he was ordered to fire upon. He tried to imagine the faces of those he might kill, but could only remember flashes from training films and blurred images of dead Vietnamese he had seen on television newscasts. Then the images became Kathy's face, and he sat up in bed, sweating but cold.

Just tell her you can't marry her, he thought, and then you won't have to hurt her later on. It had been different before.... A few months ago he had been sure there was a future for them. But now it seemed to him that Mrs. Manderson might have been right. Even his own mother, who slowly lost her idealism but not her pride while living those long years on 160 acres of the reservation, had mostly listened in silence when Mrs. Manderson said she would never allow Kathy to marry him.

Soon after that, his mother had sold off the horses, leased the meadows and pasture to Amos Spearhunter's brother, and moved into town to take a job at the Safeway store.

As he drove into the ranch, Runner saw the empty-looking fields clotted with hay bales. Between the fields and sky lay a thin border of yellow mirage, like a memory of ripe grass flooding the meadows when he first arrived home. A rubber-tired hayrack was hitched to a tractor in front of the machinery shed. When he parked near the house, Runner looked around for Kathy, but saw only her father, who was standing just inside the shed as he talked with someone hidden by a long gash of shadow.

"Here he is," Mr. Manderson called. "John looks all ready to start stacking bales." A man of only medium height, Manderson gave the impression of being much larger. He had huge hands and arms, and his clothes—Big Smith overalls and blue chambray shirt like those the Navy issued—always looked freshly washed, even if he had been taking apart a greasy piece of machinery.

The other, much-younger man rose from a squatting position by the wall. He was taller than Manderson, but walked a little hunched-over at the shoulders. He had long, curving sideburns. His cheekbones protruded like his forehead, nose, and chin, so that the eyes seemed deeply sunken. He wore a faded fatigue cap, Levis, and an Army shirt with dark swatches on the sleeves where stripes had recently been taken off. His combat boots still showed patches of heavy polish on the toes.

"You know Ed Harwell, don't you?" Mr. Manderson said. "Just got out of the service a week ago. Been in Germany."

Runner nodded, remembering where he had seen the face before.

"Heard of you," Harwell said. "Guess we never really met."

They shook hands stiffly. Ed Harwell had been the soldier whose picture Runner had seen in the Mandersons' living room when he started going out with Kathy. Later she had written Harwell that she was breaking up with him, but neither his memory of the picture or the face of the man he just met explained very much about their relationship. Probably it didn't matter now anyway, he told himself.

"Ed's going to work for me this summer until he decides what he wants to do," said Manderson.

Harwell pulled down the brim of his cap and squinted into the sun. "Might as well start," he said to no one in particular. "Shouldn't take long to stack what's baled so far. Not with three working. Feel good to get some exercise."

"John here has been getting plenty, I guess," Kathy's father said. "That war's a damn shame. Looks like all you boys are either going off to the service or getting out."

Harwell laughed. "Better to be getting out. Or maybe just burn the old draft card and slope out to Saskatchewan."

They were walking to the hayrack when Runner saw Kathy standing by the front door to the house, her white blouse striking his eyes like a mirror's reflection. She raised one hand and smiled to him before going back inside. For an instant he imagined she was still standing there. He suddenly wanted to call out to her, before it was too late—tell her everything he had known and felt earlier was becoming confused during the leave, that he needed badly to talk with her.... But she was gone. He was staring into willows along the riverbank, where rust-colored steers scrubbed their necks on an old fence post and bawled sadly.

"Which ones do you want?" Ed Harwell was saying. He held out two pairs of hay hooks.

Their curved, pointed tips reminded Runner of the bayonets issued for basic training. "It doesn't matter," he said.

Harwell shrugged. "I'll use the pair with less curve. I'm taller, so I'll buck-up bales to you after we get the first layer on the hayrack. That suit you?"

"It's all right with me," Runner said. Manderson seemed pleased to have Harwell working for him, and he wondered how Kathy felt about it. The thought crossed his mind that even if he didn't break up with her, she might grow tired of waiting for him, become lonely, or discover she still cared for Harwell. But he didn't really feel jealous, and he decided this was another way his being in the Army had changed him.

After riding through cropped meadows, the two younger men began picking up bales. They were heavy—native hay mixed with clover and secured tightly with wire. When Runner snapped his hay hook into an eighty-pound bale, the sound was like a shingle breaking and the jar ran up into his shoulder. The first few seemed the worst. Each bale had to be spiked with a hook, dragged several feet, hooked again, lifted, and swung thudding onto the hayrack.

The tractor pulled its load slowly through the fields; the sun seemed to move closer as it rose; bits of grass stems, hay leaves, and dust blew into Runner's face. But the work took on a rhythm in the hook's flash in the sun and sharp, solid pound into the bales. The meadows were cleanly stripped, and new growth for the second cutting was already standing up where it had been run over by the baler. John Runner had trouble believing that a few weeks before, on his twenty-first birthday, he had been firing an M16 rifle at human-shaped silhouettes. This valley in Wyoming was his home, and like his father before him, he had grown up within sight of the high, glacier-slashed granite mountains beyond the Wind River. He hated to think of leaving. The country would always cut like a knife in some corner of his mind... as would the thought of Kathy being here without him....

When the first load was on the hayrack, Mr. Manderson drove the tractor to the stack yard. Harwell hooked the bales as Runner slid them down, and Manderson began stacking them. They worked steadily all morning until the second load of bales had been put up. After they sat down in the shade of the hayrack, no one spoke at first. Their faces were reddened from the heat and irritation of hay dust, so that they seemed feverish.

"What was it like in Germany, Ed?" Manderson asked, sucking on a grass stem. "Last war I was in the Navy and didn't see anything except the damned Atlantic Ocean."

"Wasn't bad. Hate to be a German, though. Hard to believe people can live that way. They got a lock for everything they own. Almost as soon as the sun goes down, they start locking up."

Manderson smiled and twisted one corner of his mouth as he tried to dislodge a piece of hay with his tongue. "Women?" he asked at last, pleased by the joke.

Harwell was unbuttoning the front of his shirt to brush hay leaves from his skin. "All kinds—good and bad. As far as the ones a GI would meet, I'd say mostly looking for a ticket to the States." He glanced at Runner, as if remembering something which amused him. "After Kathy and me broke up, I decided to give it a try with one of them. A man gets to feeling like that after a while over there. So we got set up in a room near the post and I started learning a little German talk."

"Good-looking, I suppose," said Manderson.

"She sure wasn't the kind you'd kick out of bed." Harwell pulled his billfold from a hip pocket and opened it ceremoniously.

The picture they saw was indistinct and yellowing from poor development—the girl thin and overdressed, standing at the corner of a dirty stone building. The girl's image made Runner feel a vague sense of sorrow and loss.

Manderson examined the picture closely and slapped Harwell on the back. "Guess you did learn some German!"

"Too much maybe," said Harwell. "Got pregnant on me after a year and started talking marriage—about coming to the States and what-all we were going to do together. You bet I moved out fast then. With a girl like that, there's no telling whose kid it was. For a while she kept coming around and talking about killing herself, but I'd already sworn off foreign women."

Manderson was returning the billfold when the dinner gong rang at the ranch house. As Runner stood up and moved out of the shade, he realized how tired his shoulders were from handling the bales. He wondered what Kathy had liked about Harwell when they were going together. Had it been something different from what she found to love in him? It could turn out he and Ed Harwell were quite a bit more alike than he wanted to admit.

The noon meal was served in the kitchen. Kathy brought the dishes of food to the table in warm china bowls, while Mr. Manderson cut the pot roast. At the far end of the table, Kathy's mother sat holding a striped gray tomcat in her lap.

"Did you forget the ice tea?" she called to Kathy. "You always forget something when there's company."

"Let her alone." Manderson winked at his daughter. "Can't you see she's flustered with so many young men here at once."

"Don't tease me, Dad," Kathy said. Her face was tinted scarlet from working over the stove, and she smiled at Runner.

"Why not," her father said. "Ed and John don't mind."

"Don't you mind, Runner?" Mrs. Manderson always spoke his last name as if it were the only name he had.

"You're all letting the food get cold," Kathy said quickly, starting the dishes around. "The men are hungry, Mother."

The marble eyes of the cat stared yellowly up at Runner over the table top. Mrs. Manderson's face had the same look of bored power. Her bleached hair was in rollers and bound up tightly in a scarf. Although obviously well past forty, she wore a blue halter and tight black bell-bottoms. Her skin was deeply tanned—such a heavy brown that it looked unhealthy. Even when they started eating she kept the cat on her lap, and its tail beat nervously against the table.

"Why don't you put that damn cat down," Manderson said. "You know I don't like him around at meals."

"He's not hurting anything. You never pay any attention to the things *I* don't like." She turned to Harwell. "Does Tom bother you, Ed? Somebody around here should be on my side."

"No, he don't. Not much that does bother me, I guess."

"You see!" Mrs. Manderson told her husband. "You and Kathy can't gang up on me this time."

"Nobody's ganging up on you. You just imagine that."

"They always do," she explained to Harwell. "They both hate me."

Runner found he wasn't hungry. She hadn't been this hostile in front of him before, and he supposed it was for Ed's benefit.

"Please, Mother," said Kathy. "You promised we wouldn't argue today."

Mrs. Manderson had stopped eating already and lit a cigarette. "Well, your father started it. He's angry with me about something, but won't tell me what I've done."

Manderson's mouth tightened. "You know what it is. Do you want me to say it?"

His wife angrily pushed the cat from her lap. "Go ahead. Runner knows what I think about him going with our daughter. As far as I'm concerned, he's a dog-eating Indian just like his jailbird brother. If you had any guts, you'd take the shotgun and run him off this place...."

In the silence that followed, Mrs. Manderson got up from the table. The rest of the sentence came as a scream just before the kitchen door slammed shut. "But you don't have any guts!"

Runner excused himself and went outside. He could hear Manderson talking to Ed Harwell. Then he heard the back door bang.

"Shall we take a walk?" Kathy stood watching him, her hands thrust in the pockets of her Levis. "It's cooler by the river now."

"Maybe it would be quieter too," he said.

She began to pull him by the hand. "Everything's nicer there."

Runner let her lead him away from the house, through the ripening chokecherry bushes, and under old cottonwoods. A dove fluttered against the leaves as if trapped by a net. The larger trees blocked out sunlight, and the air smelled of moist earth and the slough across the river overhung with stunted willows, whose tops splayed out limply into dead, brown-scummed water.

"Please don't be angry," Kathy said. "She's been in a cruddy mood."

"I'm not angry." He made himself smile. "Anyhow, you know Indians aren't supposed to show what they feel. No one can tell if we're angry or happy."

When she thought he was joking, Kathy's face relaxed a little. "It's not so much you personally that makes her act that way. She still thinks... Well, that it's wrong to let me marry someone with Indian blood."

"Plenty of people around here agree with her," Runner said.

"She's worse than most of them."

"Maybe. What makes her so angry about it?"

Kathy hesitated. "I'm not sure...."

But Runner thought she did know. He noticed that her hair was the color of ripe brome grass growing near the river.

"Do you remember the first summer you worked here?" she asked.

"I don't remember anything about that. It must have been someone else you're thinking of."

"When I asked your name, you said John Slow Runner, and I wouldn't believe you."

"I thought you should know."

"I didn't laugh to hurt you, but you would hardly speak to me all summer. I decided you didn't like girls."

"I was busy with the hay," he said. "Besides, I thought you were Ed Harwell's girl when I saw that picture of him. And your mother didn't like—"

"I think I had to ask you to take me out," she interrupted.

"Yes.... You did the first time anyway."

"You're still shy, aren't you?" Kathy walked backward down the path, pulling his hand. "I thought the Army might change you. I don't want it to."

When he didn't answer, she looked hurt for a moment before crying out, "Come and race me! I'll beat you to the old cottonwood."

It was a game they had played before. She ran ahead of him, laughing and flat-footed in the moccasins he bought for her from an elderly Arapaho woman whose beadwork his father had admired. He chased Kathy through patches of sunlight and under shadowy trees. He forgot the stiffness in his body as he ran and felt his lungs working. Momentarily everything seemed simple and beautiful as he moved through feathery grass and foxtail. It was the same sensation he used to have playing basketball, when he drove in for a layup and felt the delight of capabilities no longer limited by himself or the other players.

He caught Kathy before reaching the old tree, and she turned into his arms, breathing hard and laughing warm against his neck until they both stood silently together, listening to a flicker chip into a rotting willow across the river.

"I should have told you Ed was back," she said. "But I didn't think it would matter. You don't mind his working for Dad, do you?"

He didn't mind now, but he wasn't sure how much it might matter later on. "Mostly I was surprised to see him here this morning," he said. "Your mother and father both like him, don't they?"

"Yes, but you don't have to worry," she said slowly. "Can you believe me? It's not the same with you as it was with Ed. . . . He was several years ahead of me in high school and going into the service. It started like that. I felt sorry for him because most of the girls his age were married. With you it was different."

Runner stripped leaves from a small willow and then let them flutter down one by one from his hand. "You knew I'd probably have to go in the Army too. Did you feel sorry for me?"

"No, I didn't," she said.

On the way back to the house, they stopped to watch carp fanning water over moss-softened rocks in a big pool, where one huge cottonwood grew out over the river. Light through the trees spotted the pool in irregular patterns where carp drifted slowly, almost translucent until they became shadows again.

"When I was little, I thought the carp were beautiful," Kathy said. "We've been having them seined out this summer to save the trout. That's why the slough smells so bad. They throw the dead carp over there."

Runner dropped a rock into the pool, and the carp were gone. Like his leave. Like the couple dead in a Fourth-of-July accident caused by his brother. Like the half-wild Indian horses sometimes killed on the highway. Most people said the horses didn't have any business running loose... looming up fiery-eyed in headlights of cars driven by out-of-state tourists hurrying to reach town before all the motels were full. And some thought Indians shouldn't be allowed to drink and then drive their secondhand automobiles and pickups over the fifteen miles of federal highway between town and the reservation. Surely the troublesome ones could find something useful to do—like making souvenirs for the tourists, working in uranium mines, fighting forest fires... or going into the service, where Indian blood didn't matter quite so much.

"It's not forever," Kathy said, certain that he too was thinking about his leave ending. "The time will go quickly. And then it will seem like you never were away. We'll walk here and look at the river again."

Only I won't want that if it means living like my father and mother or the Mandersons, he thought, watching Kathy stretch her arms out for balance as she danced over the river and back on the tree trunk. He knew that running away from her would make him another Ed Harwell—free of responsibility, safe from drawing her into a marriage of the sort that had trapped his parents.... I'll tell her this evening, he decided, and then afterward we won't have to see each other. He could leave for the new camp a few days early.

They were walking along the edge of an oat field, where Runner saw magpies clustered around a dead sheep. Squalling from long bills, they fluttered and hopped over the woolly hump. Kathy threw a stone at the birds, flipping her arm the same way a boy would.

"Someday you'll be out of the Army," she said, "and I won't have to write letters to a strange camp or foreign country.... I know we won't change too much before you're back."

"How can you be so sure?"

She was smiling at him. "You want me to be sure, don't you?"

He hesitated, starting to tell her what he had decided... but unable to. "Yes," he lied. And he told himself it hadn't been the right time.

The work in the afternoon became harder. Air didn't move, and when they stopped to rest, the only sound other than the tractor's engine was a monotonous clicking of grasshoppers as they arced out of the stubble. The ranch buildings shimmered far away, distorted by heat waves.

A large hawk hunted low over an irrigation ditch. Runner saw the weaving motions of its head as the bird searched for movement along the grassy bank. He kept thinking of Ed Harwell as he told about the German girl, and Mrs. Manderson watching her husband and stroking the tomcat during the noon meal. He knew it must be hard on Kathy to see her parents fighting because of him, but not discussing with her the decision about becoming a career soldier was probably just as cruel.

On the other side of the hayrack, Harwell leaned over a bale, sweating as his hook-tipped arm rose and pounded down with careless skill. Runner wondered if Harwell, despite his talk, missed Army life. He had begun to feel cheated somehow by his leave. He felt he should still be training for the booby traps, land mines, and rockets of Vietnam. Here, during his last days at home, he was faced with emotions and demands that kept pulling him in confusing directions. But I won't hurt Kathy, he told himself. I love her. I won't hurt her... I won't....

As they were taking the next load to the stack, the Manderson's black sedan passed on the road. Runner saw Kathy's mother driving by herself. She was dressed up, with her hair combed out and free of the scarf. She didn't look over at them.

"Guess you know where she's going, don't you?" Harwell asked.

"No," Runner said.

Harwell was grinning. "Thought Kathy might have told you. If Manderson's old lady can't get him to do what she wants, she goes to town and starts drinking in the bars. Sometimes she buys a couple of bottles and comes back to the ranch, or maybe she'll make him bring her home. Anyhow, she'll keep drinking and hassling and making things miserable for him until she gets her way. Some people say she isn't too particular who she picks up at the bars. Might just be talk, though. . . . She doesn't much go for you, does she?"

Fragments of hay under Runner's shirt collar itched against his skin. "No, she doesn't," he said.

"None of my business," Harwell went on. "I've known the Mandersons since high school, so I thought I'd tell you what to expect. She was the one asked me to work here this summer, maybe get into the ranching business with them. God knows they need help, but she's a hard woman to be around sometimes."

He had already guessed Kathy's mother wanted Harwell to stay on the ranch, although he didn't know the Mandersons had offered him a share in its operation. But you can't believe all of Harwell's talk, he thought, even if most of it made sense. As long as Runner had a place in Kathy's life, her mother would keep trying to break them apart. He felt the months he would be gone stretch out like a prison term for Kathy, and her mother's hatred made him wonder again why he ever believed he could marry her and make a new life for them here.

"I wouldn't want to cross her too far," Harwell said. "She's got a mean streak when things don't suit her."

The hayrack jolted and stopped beside the half-finished stack of bales. Mr. Manderson climbed off the tractor. "Two more loads should do it for today," he called out.

His voice sounded different than before, and Runner could see the hurt in his eyes. He was reminded of the way Kathy had looked when she met him outside the house after lunch.

Manderson was staring off toward the mountains. "She goes fast if a man's got help."

"Sure does," Ed Harwell said. "And after supper I'll have me the biggest beer in town. A man works up a thirst out here." He kicked bales off the hayrack and jumped long-leggedly onto the stack. Gesturing with his hay hook, he called to Runner: "Throw her down, old buddy. Quicker we start, quicker we finish."

After supper Harwell left, saying something to Mr. Manderson at the door which made him laugh bitterly. As Runner sat by the kitchen window watching Kathy clear the dishes, he saw a faint line of dust through the meadows and then a thicker, drifting plume as Harwell's car reached the county road. Her parents were getting ready to go into town also; he could hear them arguing in their bedroom. He hated the sound of their voices and felt that he should be leaving too.

"They do that until I want to scream at both of them." Kathy was putting on a cobbler-style apron, and she turned around so he could button and tie it.

The curve of her neck was brown and thin—childlike somehow, even though she was nineteen—and he thought of how young she was, and how dependent on him to help her deal with the emotional conflict within this house. But he had only made things worse.

"I wish they'd quit," she said. "They never do, though. She can't stop trying to hurt him, and he gives in to her but hates himself for it. I guess they can't help themselves."

"It's me she's upset about."

"Please don't say that. She's had spells like this before."

Color darkened in fields and trees outside. Soon Kathy's father and mother drove away. The sheep came up to a shed behind the house, and the lead ewe's bell clanged loudly with each slow step. The mountains appeared to ignite with red-orange all along their broken, jagged spine, but soon this too died out.

When Kathy finished washing the dishes, they sat on the living-room floor. She turned on the portable stereo, and the records were the ones he remembered before leaving for the Army—Johnny Cash's "Born to Lose" and a twangy, mournful song by Bobbie Gentry, "Ode to Billy Joe." The Army-camp jukeboxes always seemed to be playing rock music by groups called the Beatles, the Grateful Dead, Rolling Stones, the Experience... or "House of the Rising Sun," "In the Midnight Hour," "Light My Fire." It was as though the weeks of training had broken him from the slow rhythms of the reservation and a small town, and initiated him into sounds and attitudes from some larger but shallower life, where he could live or die in the military clothes and relationships provided for him.

One of the gray kittens wandered in from the kitchen, and Kathy began to play with it. She held the kitten against her face, and it batted her cheek with one paw. "Where's your mother, little cat," she murmured. "Gone and left you in the dark?"

The kitten caught strands of hair in its paw. She shook her head, laughing quietly, and dark hair fell across her forehead. She realized he was watching her, and she put the kitten down and turned toward him. Green light from the stereo's dial made reflections in her eyes like fragments of bright jade. She had taken off her shoes; her socks, blouse, and throat became pieces of the indistinct whiteness she formed in the dusk. There was no sound outside now except an occasional cough from one of the ewes and the river washing over rocks below the big pool.

"It's not gone yet," Kathy said, and then was embarrassed for revealing her thoughts. She stood up and came over to sit cross-legged beside him. The last record — "Gentle on My Mind" — ended abruptly. She didn't look at him but said, "If you want to, we can go upstairs. They won't be back until much later.... We can see their headlights coming on the road."

She had spoken so naturally that it took a moment for Runner to realize what she was saying. And then he was sure she wanted him to make the decision, as if she understood he might be separating himself from her. He wondered if they knew each other too well for him to carry out a betrayal which might save them both. He waited, listening to his heart beat, and heard the kitten scrambling across the kitchen floor. Then he was walking with her to the stairs, where each step was a light cry of wood and nails under her shoeless feet and then his own. At the top they both stopped awkwardly. He could see nothing except black space and a window with sky beyond. Tell her now, he thought. Tell her quickly.

"Be careful," she whispered, although there was no one to hear them. "There's a chair somewhere in front of you."

They found the bed and sat down on the edge, not touching each other. An unpleasant odor came in with the clean air from an open window.

"It's not really so long, is it?" she said. "I'll write often, and the time will go quickly. We'll feel just the same then, won't we?"

He couldn't lie again and remained silent. To his surprise he heard her begin to cry. And he remembered how, as a boy, he had once found his mother out by the corral, crying quietly, after her sister's one-week visit spent near but never on the reservation.

"Most people don't know what it's like not to be able to really believe in anyone . . . even your own mother. That's the only reason I ever went with Ed. . . . I . . . I wanted to think there was someone I could believe in."

That was what Runner once thought he wanted, too. His eyes had adjusted enough to the dark that he could make out the dresser by Kathy's bed. There was a picture on the dresser—in the same frame he remembered seeing in the living room during his first dates with her. But the dim figure was not Ed Harwell. The cap cocked a bit over one eye, the uniform with bloused combat boots, and the face were his own new identity.

"It's worse between my parents than it used to be," Kathy went on, her voice husky from crying. "After I started high school, she went away for a whole year. . . . But he took her back. Do you understand why he took her back?"

He shook his head, but in a way he could sympathize with Mr. Manderson, who like his own mother had tried by compromise and sacrifice to keep a family together. It was mostly John Runner who still eluded him, and he stared again at the picture.

"Why does your mother hate me so much?" he asked suddenly. "Is it just because I'm a half-breed?"

Kathy didn't answer.

He thought she had been shocked by his using the word himself. "We used to joke about it. Remember?"

"Maybe we shouldn't have," she finally said. "Her family... my mother's.... They had Indian blood, and she's always been afraid people would find out. I'm almost as much a half-breed as you are."

Runner imagined that one of the steel hay hooks was being driven up through his stomach and probing for his heart. He felt completely alone. "You're sure about your mother?" he asked.

"She wishes with all her tainted heart and soul it wasn't so, but it's true enough.... I know I should have told you before."

"Why didn't you?"

"I'm not sure," she said. "Mother made me promise not to talk about it, and I was afraid of what she'd do.... I was going to tell you, though. I've never been ashamed like her."

"You're nothing like her," Runner said.

"Not that way at least. Are you angry with me?"

He wasn't angry. He could begin to see how believing Kathy was white had made it easier to blame others for his own doubts about himself and marrying her. Like his thoughts of staying in the Army, it had given him an excuse for not risking with her the failure he had seen in the lives of his mother and father—and now suddenly it was gone. Whatever he did or didn't do with her would be as a man not white or Indian, who had the same choice of freedom and ties as Manderson and Ed Harwell... or his own father. This realization was frightening, and he instinctively wanted to escape. But here, in Kathy's dark room, he couldn't run away from himself.

A breeze had come up from the direction of the mountains, and he recognized the odor of the willow-shrouded slough where dead carp from the river were thrown. But mixed with it was the smell of grass beginning to grow again in the meadows at the end of haying season....

"Something is wrong, isn't it," Kathy said. "Have I messed up everything for us?"

He could see her lying curled across the bed, uncertain and withdrawn because of his hesitation. "No," he said. "Nothing's wrong now."

"You're sure?"

"Yes.... Shall I close the window?"

"If you want to," she said.

He decided to leave the window open. Then he lay on the bed beside her and reached out to touch her face. And he could almost believe that when car lights turned off the road from town, the leave would not be over.

The next morning when Runner drove up to the machinery shed, only Ed Harwell was waiting to start work. It was cloudy above the mountains, as though there might be rain by afternoon, but there was only one more field to finish before all the bales were stacked. When he left Kathy the night before, the Mandersons hadn't gotten back to the ranch. Now he saw their sedan parked in front of the house. He guessed they had ended their fight one way or another. Mostly he was thinking about Kathy as her body bent beneath him... her touch and movement when her arms were around him, as if holding something even his leaving would not take away.

"Looks like just you and me for a while," Harwell said. "Maybe it was too big a night for the Mandersons. They were still going strong when I left the bars about midnight."

Runner wasn't really interested in them. "Why don't you drive the tractor," he said, picking up the hay hooks he'd used the day before.

"We'll take it slow," Harwell said. "I got pretty well stoned myself. Been celebrating too hard, I guess, but it's damn good to be out of the Army."

Runner looked toward the house. The window of Kathy's bedroom was still open. He could imagine her asleep in the rumpled bed, waking up as sunlight lay across her skin. He would see her at noon... and tonight they would go off from the ranch and be together where they could talk. There was a lot for them to talk about before he left.

"Manderson told me you're probably going to 'Nam," Harwell said. "I got lucky. Can't say I envy you over in those rice paddies."

He knew he was going to feel different about it now, but it wasn't something he wanted to get into with Harwell. "I don't have much choice. You didn't either."

"Maybe not. I'm just happy I wasn't getting my ass shot off like some of the guys I had basic training with." Ed Harwell took the other pair of hay hooks from the wall of the shed. "Seeing how fucked-up the service is, I'd hate to buy it over there for nothing. But I don't wish you any bad luck, like what happened to your brother."

He wondered whether Harwell was trying to made him angry. Probably Kathy's mother had been talking to him last night in one of the bars. "You ready to start on the hay," he said.

"Sure, sure I am. I just thought we were on Indian time this morning. But if you're in a hurry, that's fine by me." He laughed. "Manderson's old lady sure isn't colorblind, is she?"

"What did she say to you?"

"About the same thing she was telling everybody yesterday at lunch. And I guess she'd like Kathy and me to get back together. That's no big surprise, is it?"

"No," he said.

"Anyway, she was sure tying one on. She got after Manderson again to tell you to stay away from Kathy. He said he wouldn't, and they had another big blowup right there in the Avalon Bar. She was talking about leaving him like she did once before. Even asked me to pick a fight with you, say something to stir up a little trouble."

For as long as Runner could remember, he had heard bad things said, at school and around town, about his father and mother, Indians in general, about his brother and himself. Ed Harwell had enough reasons not to like him. He felt his right hand tighten around the handle of the hay hook.

Harwell was looking at him, but it was almost as though Runner was no longer there. "You know, I could tell you plenty about Kathy and me when we were together. She liked me a whole lot and..."

He was standing close enough. The steel hook would reach Harwell's throat as easily as a heavy bale up on the hayrack. It angered him that Kathy would be dragged into this by her mother and Ed Harwell. He was angry with them for believing his feeling for her could be changed by anything they said or did to him. He was angry with his family, whose lives he could neither accept or change... and with himself for allowing the leave, like his own life so far, to slip away while decisions were made for him.

"Go on," he said. "I'm listening."

Harwell stood watching him in a different way. Finally he shook his head and laughed as if he'd been making a joke all along. "It don't matter. Kathy's a good kid, but we never would of married. Guess I got too wide a wild streak to suit her. I can't see me settling down on this ranch, or anywhere else for a while. I told her old lady so last night. She didn't like it much, but I can't help that."

The hay hooks hung loosely from Runner's hands. There was silence around the shed and house, and then cattle lowing as they left the water to graze... the noise of magpies from over by the slough. His anger was gone. For some reason, he remembered his father's face when he came quietly into their house after an all-night peyote meeting. Runner knew he probably wouldn't have struck Harwell with the hay hook. He planned to survive his remaining months in the Army, though, and come back here. He and Kathy would find a way for themselves. It wasn't much to be sure of, but maybe it would be enough.

He stood watching Ed Harwell walk away to the hayrack, fasten his hooks to the frame with a piece of baling wire, and then climb onto the tractor. He started the engine, and Runner thought he had given it too much gas, making it backfire. But Harwell was looking toward the house. Then Runner recognized the sound too and ran out of the shed.

Kathy was at the upstairs window calling out something to him. He ran faster toward the front door of the house, seeing a blur of pale trees along the river in the distance. He wasn't breathing hard but running well, as though making a cut on the basketball court or beginning the obstacle course in basic training... not knowing he was too late until the door opened and he saw Mrs. Manderson, hair wild around her face on the stock of the shotgun, the blast loud enough to fill his ears forever.

MORNING FLIGHT

HEADNOTES FOR "MORNING FLIGHT"

OF THE STORIES in this collection, "Morning Flight" is the most recent to be published and in the time of its main setting, the middle of World War II, the earliest. That war as it began in Europe would have been going on for three years when Ray, "the boy" at the center of this story, had his twelfth birthday. "Morning Flight" and "Leave's End" are both stories narrated in third person with a strong focus on the lives and thinking of the two central characters. The differences between the perceptions of a preadolescent boy like Ray and John Runner, a young man of mixed racial heritage, became one of my concerns in handling the characterization and narrative voice in "Morning Flight."

This story involved a boy growing up during the century's most widespread and significant war, reported through radio, newsreels, movies, newspapers, magazines, and books with an immediacy entirely new in American life. Ray would have been nine when the war started and fifteen when it ended. Without living during that war, I couldn't have written the background for this story in the way I did. "Morning Flight" is the most autobiographical of the eight stories collected here in some of the boy's feelings about hunting, his future, his family, and his desire to no longer be treated as a child even though he often feels like one. But the story is not creative nonfiction or memoir. Ray is ultimately a fictional creation as are the other characters, the closely related events that occur, the shades of meaning that emerge from the characters and what happens to them, and other aspects of the story. Along with the enjoyment reading a story or novel can give us, fiction has its own kind of truth.

A very early draft of "Morning Flight" was written during a sabbatical leave in the 1970s, and I was able to show another version of it to my father, who had taught me to hunt, while he was still alive. The story had always been long. Whenever I made revisions it became even longer though also improved, as usually happens. Its length seemed to work against publication. When I shortened the story as much as possible, it became clearer and tighter, but I knew something still wasn't quite right. After I had retired from teaching and published a volume of Wyoming poems, *The Ranch*, I took out "Morning Flight" again and rewrote some parts of it and retyped the manuscript. I put it away while I worked on other projects.

Sometime later I received an issue of the *South Dakota Review* which had a beautiful duck decoy on the cover. The longer I looked at it, the more memories came back of decoys spread out and moving quietly on a lake in early morning light... and the story I had written about the boy, his family, the war during which he was growing up, and what he learned of love, death, and the loss of childhood. I dug out "Morning Flight" and without further revisions mailed the manuscript to the editor of *South Dakota Review*, Brian Bedard, who had worked at *Quarterly West* twenty years earlier when "Winter Days Are Long" was published there. The only change I made after the manuscript had been accepted was adding two sentences in the final paragraph when the story was in galley proof. "Morning Flight" appeared in the Fortieth Anniversary Issue of *South Dakota Review* published in 2003.

MORNING FLIGHT

He was twelve. His birthday had been two months ago, not long after the family's summer vacation in northern Wyoming, trout fishing high among pines and quaking aspen. That was their last trip together before his brother left for Navy boot camp, and it had been difficult to make the drive because of gasoline rationing. In a way, the boy enjoyed being the only son left at home, though he kept this feeling hidden from his mother and father. It was hard to explain, and he sometimes worried about acting like a selfish child. Carl was nineteen and going off to "the war," while his own summer passed slowly through days of sun and heat, the certainty against his feet of hot concrete edging the VFW swimming pool at Memorial Park... his pleasure in having the bedroom to himself after his brother left.

"Why do you stay alone so much?" his mother had asked after school started. "We've lived in Wyoming for nearly a year now. Are you still having trouble making friends?"

"I have friends," he answered.

"Then why don't you invite them over? I can't understand why you wouldn't let me give a birthday party for you. Now that you're in junior high here, you'll want to do more things with your friends."

He remembered how the thought of girls in white summer dresses, subdued boys in Sunday suits, and awkward joking among stiff classmates around a picnic table covered by cake and ice cream in his back yard, had seemed unbearable. "I see them all day at school," he said. "And besides, I've been real busy lately."

His mother looked at him more carefully. "Busy," she repeated. "What keeps you so busy, Ray?"

Her smile made him uneasy. He was becoming wary of the way his answers to her questions formed a pattern she found revealing and sometimes unsettling. "You know," he said, "with the model airplanes, and Dad and I . . . the decoys."

She nodded. "Yes, the decoys—I've noticed. The decoys and those old hunting-and-fishing magazines. I just hope you aren't getting behind in your schoolwork."

That was safer ground and he met her eyes. His mother's hair had begun to gray, but the boy thought she was beautiful. "You saw my grades last spring. I'm not having any trouble keeping up."

"Well . . . I hope you aren't." She had turned away as if not entirely satisfied. "You've been so quiet since Carl left."

"I'm really okay," he had said. "You don't have to worry about me."

Which was true, the boy decided. The model airplanes were part of his childhood, when he had spent long hours making solid replicas of his favorite planes—the Grumman Wildcat, Hawker Hurricane, and the P-40 used by the Flying Tigers in China. Now he and a few other seventh and eighth graders made ugly black models for the Army Air Corps to use in identification training. It wasn't an interest any more but an assignment, and he had difficulty making planes which would pass the exact inspection of the shop teacher.

The decoys were different. His father had once belonged to a duck-hunting club in California which gave him two-dozen old wooden decoys when the oil company he worked for sent him to West Texas. They were battered, flecked with stray shot, broken-eyed, with rusty keels and loose heads. Paint had been worn and scaled until only the body and head shapes suggested the breeds of ducks being imitated. But the blocks were solid cedar and had been made much more carefully than the new decoys of wood fiber or plastic.

During the first year of the war, his father, a petroleum engineer, had been transferred to Casper, Wyoming. He was in charge of his company's oil-drilling operations over a large area of the Rocky Mountains. The boy had become used to his father's working long hours and often being gone on weekends. In the earlier war, he had been in the Army in France, but now he was "essential" and didn't have to go into the service again. The fathers and brothers of some of the boy's friends had been gone for a year or more, and he assumed that he too would join up someday just like Carl, only he would be in the Air Corps not the Navy.

As the hunting season grew nearer, the boy and his father had begun working on the decoys. They removed the old lead weights and started scraping away the remaining paint. One evening they sat together at the dining-room table with a catalog from Herter's and made out an order for decoy paints, new glass eyes, keels, and anchors. The paint order was complicated since the decoys were mixed species—mallard drakes and hens, pintails, teal, bluebills...a few canvasbacks. While waiting the long three weeks for the supplies, he and his father had sandpapered the decoys and reglued their heads.

"It's too bad there's no dove-hunting season in Wyoming," the boy said as they worked through a Saturday afternoon and listened to football games and news broadcasts on the radio.

His father was relighting his pipe. When the boy was younger, he thought his father had the appearance of an Indian—a high, long nose and thin mouth, thick black hair—but his features were no longer so narrow. Actually he had put on too much weight, the boy knew from conversations between his parents. Yet his mother called him an unusually handsome man when she worried out loud about attractive young secretaries at his office, or the "affairs" of other men in the oil business. The boy had a hazy conception of what exactly constituted an "affair," but assumed it was somehow connected with hotel rooms, honky-tonks, whiskey drinking...and love, a subject adults never seemed to discuss with consistency. Certainly he himself, he had decided, looked little like his father. He was much shorter and thicker in the hips, resembling his mother.

"It's too bad about the doves," his father said. "There are deer and antelope, though. I've heard there's pheasant shooting in the eastern part of the state. But you were getting good on doves last year. We'll both miss that kind of hunting."

The boy nodded, thinking about their last hunt together before they moved from Texas.

He and his father had driven out to a stock tank edged by tall mesquite. They were the only ones there, and his father had shown his trust by letting him take a stand on the opposite side of the tank. An hour before dusk the doves had begun coming in, flying incredibly fast until right over the water and then changing direction, slowing, or zigzagging at impossible angles. He tried to be careful of his ammunition—there was a shortage that had become worse as the war continued. His twenty-eight-gauge pump had been given to him the year before on his birthday, and he did well enough when doves were crossing at right angles, small and streamlined against the flat-blue sky, their wings often appearing swept back like those of an Airacobra fighter model he was building.

The boy had to be careful to mark down the birds he killed, for their dun, lightly iridescent feathers blended into the clay and dead grass around the tank. In his hands the doves were light and warm. He loved them and the darkening autumn evening in a way he could express to no one, even his father, who had taught him to respect the skill and beauty of the game he sought.

His father's shotgun became quiet, and the next thing the boy knew he was walking toward him from the tank's rim. At that moment a dove came in straight above the boy's head, wobbling and unnerving, the kind of shot he had been missing all evening. He didn't wait too long this time, but blotted away the bird with the end of the moving barrel and fired. To his surprise the dove dropped down from a light puff of feathers.

The boy looked back at his father and smiled. "I guess you have your limit now," he said, when he had smoothed the dove's feathers and put it into his shooting vest.

"Not quite. But I think it's time to stop, don't you?"

It didn't sound like a test of his age—the sort of question his father had once asked in order to evaluate the boy's answer. It was only his mother who still displayed openly her doubts about his judgment.

"Yes, it's fine with me," he said. "Besides, we'll have the birds to clean when we get home. I bet Carl will be sorry he didn't come with us."

His father nodded, preoccupied with his own thoughts.

As they hiked back to the car, the boy said, "I'm glad you brought me. Doves are hard to hit and I wasn't sure how I would do."

"It was a nice shot, son. I couldn't have done better myself."

The boy was pleased, and his father's hunting coat had seemed to turn golden in the final light before sundown....

Remembering the dove hunt made him happy, and he hoped it had strengthened his role as a hunting companion. He picked up a pintail hen and ran his fingers over the decoy's shattered eyes. "Carl will be finished with boot camp next month, won't he?"

"It looks that way. He's having a tough time of it now, though. They've got him working his tail off."

"Didn't Carl say he liked the Navy?" the boy asked.

His father laughed in an odd way. "We better talk to him about that when he's home on leave. He'll have grown up a lot by the time boot camp's over."

"I guess so," the boy said uncertainly. In Texas he had seen *I Wanted Wings*, an exciting movie about flight training at Randolph Field, and his father's comments on military life were confusing. Shifting to familiar ground, he said, "Maybe Carl will be able to go hunting while he's home."

Carl had been duck hunting many times, and it was always humiliating for the boy to be home with his mother until the two hunters returned in late afternoon with ducks to clean and muddy hip boots smelling of marsh grass and damp blinds. He had tried to accept his disappointment by carrying his father's ducks into the back yard and admiring each mallard or pintail as the picking began. But as he had grown older and finally reached his eleventh birthday, it became more difficult to be left behind. Now as they worked together with the decoys, the boy wanted badly to ask the question which would end his suspense about the approaching duck season. He knew it was simple enough—would his father be taking him this year? But he could not face the enormity of being told, "No, but we'll think about it for next year," or even worse, "We'll see, son," so that the uncertainty would continue, overshadowed by doubts about his worthiness.

His father shifted position in his chair and began knocking burned tobacco from his pipe. "The decoy paint should be here soon. We'll have our work cut out for us then."

The boy gazed through the front window at the faded-green lawn and said, "I guess we will. Painting those decoys should be a lot of fun, though," and he hoped he wasn't telling a lie.

The heavy box from Herter's arrived one afternoon while the boy was at school. It was there by the front door when he got home, but of course it wasn't his to open. He made himself a peanut-butter sandwich and a glass of Ovaltine to take to his room. Carl's neatly made bed still took up almost half the space, but the boy already thought of the room as his own. His model airplanes covered the dresser top, and despite his mother's efforts he had let his clothes occupy more and more of the closet. His brother had told him to use his Wilson Squire tennis racket and his hip boots for fishing or hunting trips. He had been awfully nice, and this too made the boy uneasy without knowing why.

He lay on his bed and finished reading a story in one of his father's outdoor magazines. It was about hunting ducks and geese in Illinois before the turn of the century. The pictures were sepia-toned scenes of half-cleared fields, a flat lake with run-down cabins where young men with mustaches held huge strings of ducks, or waterfowl filling the sky above a grain field. He had read the story before, but enjoyed it again because of his expectations about the coming duck season.

Later he completed his homework in science and world history. He was usually a good student, though much better in English than math. His mother had been right in worrying about his schoolwork recently, but if he was having trouble concentrating, he had managed to adjust by studying harder. He wasn't lazy, he told himself. No, it was more that he wanted to keep to himself some of the time and think about things which really interested or even puzzled him.

Underneath the underwear and socks in one of Carl's dresser drawers, hidden beneath the lining paper, was a picture cut from a discarded calendar—deep blue... an ocean shore at night, the naked, pale form of a dark-haired woman running from the silvery water. He had found the picture by accident soon after his brother left. The woman's curving form and whiteness brushed by shadow seemed a confirmation of what he had seen and heard from adults and his friends, beneath the surface of certain movies and schoolyard jokes, magazine photographs of actresses, and glimpses of a pretty cousin one summer during a vacation visit. But now he felt involved in the knowledge, as though this woman was familiar and soon he would know why she was coming from the sea to meet him. And he wondered what the picture had meant to Carl, who had gone with several girls in high school, but concealed the image of this woman so carefully from the family.

After dinner that evening, he helped his father unpack small cans of paint, shiny keels, and circular anchors. There was also a chart that showed where various colors of paint were to be applied.

"It does look like a lot of work," the boy finally said, when everything had been laid out on the living-room carpet for inspection.

The room smelled of pipe tobacco kept moist with apple slices in the humidor on the mantelpiece. It was one of several odors—like Hoppe's bore solvent and shaving cream—the boy always associated with his father. From where he sat he could see the glass-fronted gun cabinet at one end of the dining room and, inside, the dull-blue steel and soft glowing walnut of his father's Browning over-and-under. It was the kind of shotgun he too would own someday, along with a leg-of-mutton case and a hickory cleaning rod packed with swabs, oil, and solvent in a flat metal box.

"I'm afraid we won't get started tonight," his father was saying. "Something's come up. You don't mind postponing this decoy work for a day or so, do you?"

The boy did mind, very much, yet knew it was foolish to feel that way. There's nothing to worry about, he told himself. They would still be working together on the decoys. All his father had said was that they couldn't begin tonight.

"Today I met someone who wants to help us lease the duck lake," his father said. "His name is Tom Ryan, and he's a sergeant stationed out at the base."

The Army Air Base was a newly constructed field west of Casper, where bomber crews took their final training in clumsy-looking B-24 Liberators. Sometimes planes had crashed on bombing runs and while taking off or landing, and there were always off-duty Air-Corps men around the town. The boy hadn't known any of them personally, though.

"Do you need anyone else?" he asked. "I thought the club already had enough members to pay for hunting there."

His father stood up. "It's not that simple, son. Tom Ryan and his friends from the base went to see Clete Moore about hunting at the lake. Clete told them about our club, and Ryan called me this morning about their becoming members."

"You could say no," the boy argued. "Just because they want to hunt there doesn't mean the club has to let them join." He felt upset...threatened in a way he could not define. The half-dozen men in the duck club he knew well. They were friends of his father—a geologist, two landmen employed by his father's company, a recently divorced lawyer, an independent oil-lease broker whose son was in his junior-high class, and a men's wear clerk who was 4-F and sometimes took the boy rabbit hunting. He went target shooting with others in the club, and they all had spent social evenings at his house.

His father had been trying to convince them to hunt ducks with more fairness and discipline. Some of them were used to sneaking up on a quiet bend of the Platte River and potting birds on the water. His father kept talking about the pleasure of hunting from blinds with decoys, letting birds work to a duck call and sweep down into reasonable range before taking them on the wing. And with the formation of the club and leasing of a fine lake from a rancher near Glenrock, the boy was looking forward to hunting with men in whose presence he felt comfortable. Now his father was talking of strangers coming in—and even before he had become a part of it all.

"It isn't fair," he heard himself say.

"What isn't fair, son?" His father was watching him with surprise.

"They'll spoil it. I know I probably sound dumb, but it's how I feel about people we don't know hunting out there."

"You haven't hunted on the lake yourself," his father said, more calmly than the boy liked. "How can you be so sure Ryan and his friends would spoil things?"

It was going badly, he knew, but he had stepped too far to stop. "Well . . . I haven't shot ducks yet. I've hunted a lot, though, and it isn't the same with guys you don't know. And besides . . . "

I've waited all my life for this, he was thinking. I want to hunt ducks with you in the way you've said is right. I don't want anyone making it different from what it should be. But you haven't even asked me. It isn't fair. . . . It isn't. And he said, "You've never told me I could go this year."

His father looked thoughtful and began repacking the cans of paint. "You don't think it's right to let Ryan in the hunt club when you might not be hunting at all?"

It was close enough to the truth for the boy to feel his cheeks flush, but he didn't look away from his father's face. "Will you be taking me?" he asked.

"I've been thinking about it and talking with your mother. Hunting ducks this year is important to you, isn't it?"

He nodded. "Will you be taking me?" he repeated.

"I think you're old enough, and you damn sure handled a shotgun well when we hunted doves last fall. I don't believe you'll disappoint me."

"Thank you," he said, trying not to display his great relief, which would surely seem childish and reveal all his earlier insecurity.

"And tonight you can go with me to see Tom Ryan. Tomorrow we'll get started painting the decoys."

"All right," the boy said, unable now to think of an acceptable excuse or argument. "I'll get my jacket."

His father drove up Center Street and across the railroad tracks into the north part of town, an area unfamiliar to the boy. They stopped behind an old-fashioned white house. The garage had been crudely remodeled into a small apartment, but his father said servicemen were willing to pay high rents so wives might join them during the final weeks of training. The boy walked to the door behind his father, feeling out-of-place and resentful.

The man who answered their knock was still wearing his sergeant's uniform. He was bald and seemed to be of some indefinite age beyond that of the boy's P.E. teacher, who was rumored to be twenty-eight and rejected by the Marines because of a trick knee. The apartment was cramped, one room apparently, and smelled of stew and something sweetish that the boy could not identify.

"You like a beer?" Ryan asked his father after they had introduced themselves. He held a bottle in his hand.

"No thanks. We can't stay long. . . . This is my son Ray."

Ryan looked at him and then nodded curtly. "Is he hunting at the lake?"

"That's right," his father said. "Ray got to be a good shot on doves in Texas. He'll be hunting in the club this year."

The boy felt as though Ryan's pale eyes were cutting into him. The sergeant had pocked skin and small ears, and the boy was pleased that he had already decided to dislike him.

"Kids can screw up a duck hunt sometimes," Ryan said. "You like to shoot, do you?"

"I like to hunt," the boy answered.

"Ducks aren't as easy to knock down as doves. Up in Michigan we've got a hell's slough of diver ducks—cans and bluebills. You freeze your balls off hunting them on Erie or Huron. Use a big set with lots of dekes and knock the shit out of them when there's weather and a cold snap in Canada."

"Mostly mallards and pintails or widgeon come through here," his father said. "The hunting's pretty uneven I imagine, compared to your part of the country."

The boy heard Ryan say, "There's nothing out here but dust storms, snow, and wind. What a god-forsaken place to be stationed." At that moment a woman appeared on the far side of the apartment. A bathroom must have been located there, for now he could see a doorway behind her and light was caught in her long hair. She was standing with one arm along the doorjamb, and the boy could not turn away. In her brown sweater and slacks she seemed quite slender. Her skin was pale white beneath the dark hair, and she was smiling. Except for the picture in Carl's dresser drawer, he had never seen any woman that beautiful. He was certain she could not be Tom Ryan's wife—there had to be some other explanation for her being there. No one who looked like she did could be connected with the coarse-mouthed, ugly man who would not put down his beer bottle long enough to shake hands.

Ryan must have noticed her also, for he called out, "Bring me another beer, Fern. We're going to bullshit about the duck club."

The boy hoped his father would make some excuse to avoid being sociable with Ryan, but soon the two men were seated on the sofa and the woman served them beer. This time his father accepted, and they began exchanging stories of duck hunting. Even more disturbing, Tom Ryan had introduced Fern by saying they "hadn't been married long, but long enough." Just as he was feeling awkward and left out, something incredibly soft brushed the side of his face. The woman had leaned down over his shoulder and was smiling at him. He realized that the sweet smell he had noticed earlier was her perfume.

"Why don't you come in the kitchen," she said. "I'm going to have some cocoa. You'd like some too, wouldn't you?"

At first the boy was reluctant to leave his father and the talk of hunting. But he followed her, feeling more comfortable when he was seated at a white porcelain table. Actually the kitchen was only the far corner of the apartment, but he felt isolated from the two men on the sofa. A small radio on the counter, turned very low, was playing the end of "They're Either Too Young or Too Old," a popular song that he had often heard. When "Comin' In on a Wing and a Prayer" began, she turned it off. As the woman moved around putting cocoa on the stove, she occasionally brushed against his chair.

"It's hard to get," she said. "The cocoa. Because of the war. I have plenty of sugar, too."

The boy sat watching her and then turned away when he realized he was staring.

"What's the matter?" she asked. "Don't you like talking with me?"

He did like it, but found this hard to say. Finally he looked up and smiled, hoping she would understand.

She laughed. "You don't have any sisters at home, do you?"

"No," he said. "I have a brother, though—in the Navy."

"You do? A lot of my relatives and friends from high school are in the service. Some of them like the life, but I hate it. Are you in high school?"

He thought she was teasing him somehow, but it pleased him that she would think he was older. "No," he said. "I'm in junior high."

She placed their cups on the white table. Her eyes seemed greenish against her pale skin. He stirred his cocoa and looked away.

"I hated school," the woman said. "As soon as high school was over I got a job. The war had begun, and first thing I knew we were... married. Just like that!"

She didn't like being married to Ryan, the boy decided. She was too beautiful and nice to really like him—it was a mistake she now regretted. Behind him he heard Ryan's laughter and then that of his father. They sounded like old friends, and his father began talking about the decoys they were working on. The boy felt betrayed.

"Do you enjoy hunting?" the woman asked.

Her question took him by surprise. He lowered his cup, wondering why it was difficult to admit that he did. Probably his feelings were something he didn't really know how to explain to her. Yet he wanted to talk and for her to like him.

She didn't seem bothered by his not answering. "My good husband doesn't care about anything else," she said. "Ever since I've known him it's been like that. Where we lived in Michigan he had a bunch of buddies who'd been hunting together since they were kids. They were just like a family. He'd rather give me up than make them angry. Do you know what I mean?"

"Maybe I do," he said slowly. "I guess I might feel that way myself about hunting, but I wouldn't...."

The boy was both unhappy and relieved when his father called to him that it was time to go home. He thanked Ryan's wife for the cocoa. She smiled at him and winked. Once he and his father were outside the apartment, the boy glanced back and saw her standing beside Ryan in the doorway, his arm a darker streak across the front of her sweater.

"He's really not so bad once you get to know him," his father said when they were back in the car.

He's worse, the boy thought. I hate him.... How could she live with him?

"He and his friends want to join the club, son. They're a long way from home and will go overseas soon. Flying in combat with a bomber crew is dangerous as hell. They lose a lot of men."

"All right," the boy said. "I knew it would turn out this way."

"You don't mind then?"

"I don't like him," the boy said, "but it's okay. When will we start painting the decoys?"

"Tomorrow night," his father said. "We'll have to work fast from here on.... Mrs. Ryan is quite a lady, isn't she. How was the cocoa?"

"It was fine," he answered seriously. "She's very nice."

The boy had difficulty getting to sleep that night. Early in the morning he woke up feeling uncomfortable and went to the bathroom. It didn't help, and when he finally slept again, the boy dreamed of a naval battle worse than the newsreel pictures he had seen of the fighting around the Solomon Islands. When the last Japanese aircraft attack was finished, his brother's carrier was sinking, with sailors jumping off the flaming flight deck into a blood-red sea. He knew, without actually seeing it happen, that Carl had been killed ... and he was the one who must comfort the woman his brother loved, whose face was pale white and surely beautiful. ...

It took two weeks, working each evening with newspapers spread over the kitchen table, for the boy and his father to paint the two-dozen decoys. Once they finished the prime coating, the work became slow and painstaking. Each decoy required several different colors, and individual feathers on the hens had to be stroked in carefully with a small brush. Still, it was a satisfying time for the boy. While they worked together, he and his father could talk of blinds, the best way to set decoys ... shotguns and shells. And sometimes—even more important to the boy—they just remained quiet and comfortable in each other's company, the way his parents often acted when absorbed in something of mutual interest. Previously he had assumed they were bored with each other at such times. Now he wondered if his mother found the same satisfaction in his father's company that he was experiencing.

"Next Saturday's opening day," the boy said one evening. "We'll be finished by then, won't we?"

His father laughed. "It looks that way. Tomorrow we'll work on the keels and anchor cords. Some of the boys were out checking the new blinds last week. There'll be water in the pits, so you better get out your rubber boots."

"I don't have any high ones," the boy said. "But Carl told me to use his if I needed them."

His father dipped a brush into turpentine and wiped the bristles clean on a rag. "He won't have much use for them for a while. Did your mother tell you his leave's been canceled?"

"No," he said. "I thought he'd been promised a leave after boot camp."

"Usually it works that way, son. But Carl's been assigned to electronics-repair school, and the next class begins right away. He'll be stationed on the Gulf Coast. It shouldn't be too difficult for him to get home when his training's finished."

The boy was puzzled about what the assignment meant. "I thought he was going to a ship somewhere... to the war."

"It could have been that way. Your brother's always been interested in electronics, though. The Navy needs people trained to repair their new equipment, so he probably won't be in on any actual fighting. We should be grateful for that."

"What about the war you were in?" the boy asked. "You fought against the Germans, didn't you? I've heard you talk about trenches and the enemy attacking with bayonets."

His father picked up a mallard decoy and began adding the deep-blue swatches on the wings. "That's so, but not everyone in the service actually fights. Someone has to do the other jobs. And war is different now than when I was in the Army. People have to be trained to handle all kinds of complicated weapons."

The boy found it confusing to think of his brother serving in the war without fighting the enemy face-to-face. He felt guilty now, too, for having dreamed about Carl's death and being pleased he wasn't coming home for a while. His brother had sent him a sailor hat from boot camp, along with a letter about the tough training and a swimming test some recruits might never pass. No, his happiness about Carl being gone was wrong, something his mother would find very troubling and his father wouldn't accept—like the boy's disliking Sergeant Ryan and not wanting to have him hunt ducks at the lake. Sometimes he felt as though his brother and Ryan were becoming mixed up in his thinking to form a shadowy older presence that shared secrets and attitudes he might never understand. Hidden pictures, gestures—an arm carelessly thrown across a woman's breast—and words like "affair" and "sleeping together" that meant more than was said.

"When do you think the war will be over?" the boy asked. "I've heard you can join up when you're eighteen."

For a moment his father held the paintbrush very still. "It's hard to say, son. We've done pretty well in North Africa, and the Germans have bitten off more than they can chew with Russia. Things are going to be damn rough in the Pacific, but after Guadalcanal it may just be a matter of time until we invade Japan. Nobody knows for sure what will really happen, though."

The boy listened regularly with his parents to Gabriel Heatter and other radio news-commentators, and had already decided the fighting was something he would eventually experience. Being a flier was one of his recurrent daydreams, although he sometimes wondered if he might feel relieved if the war ended before he grew up. Recently he had seen the movie *So Proudly We Hail*, where Veronica Lake was a nurse who blew herself up, along with the Japanese who were capturing her, and he wondered if he would be capable of such heroism... or that of the Army sergeant facing the enemy alone at the end of *Bataan*. His own fantasies about the war were usually concerned with his doing something brave, and lately a woman was involved or waiting for him to come back. But he no longer thought the woman in Carl's calendar picture was interesting, really, despite her nakedness. Taken out from the dresser drawer, she somehow became deceptive and disappointing, unconnected with the feelings he had now, ever since the visit to Ryan's apartment....

"When we're hunting together," his father said, "be sure to keep your head down when the ducks begin working the decoys. They have sharp eyes and get scared off by a movement or seeing sunlight on your face. The pintails are especially hard to decoy in."

"I'll be careful," he said. "How can you tell the pintails from other ducks?"

"They're big like mallards, only more streamlined and slender. They have long black tail-feathers, and sometimes the drakes make a whistling sound. Often they'll circle the decoys time after time before deciding to come in."

The boy felt a cold edge of excitement working deep within his chest. He wondered how he would live through the days of school and ordinary routine separating him from his dream of opening day. Behind the bright glass of the gun cabinet, he could see his slender shotgun with its shimmering blueness, shining stock and forearm. Yet as he caressed it with his gaze, he was reminded of the woman Fern's long hair, her perfume returning to his memory as sharp as the smell of drying color on the mallard hen his father had finished painting.

Someone touched the boy's shoulder. He turned, surprised to see his mother standing behind him and smiling at them both. It was an intrusion, but unthinkable to hurt her by letting his reaction show. She seemed to grow into his back and become a heavy weight bearing down into his bones. His father appeared pleased by the interruption.

"Are you two staying up all night?" she asked. "Tomorrow is a school day, Ray."

His father stood up, and the mother moved beside him. The boy rose awkwardly and began putting away the paints.

"I'll finish cleaning up here," his father said. "Thanks for the help with the decoys."

"It's okay," he answered. "I liked doing it. Well . . . I'll see you in the morning."

They both told him good night and smiled, but he felt they were not paying much attention. It looked to be one of the nights when they made coffee and sat in the living room, talking and laughing together long after he had gone to bed. Tonight, though, he was tired and went to sleep after only a short period lying awake, imagining a sky filled with wings, calls of flocks wheeling in changing patterns above the lake . . . white-breasted pintails finally dropping down toward the deceptive wooden blocks, wings cupped like reaching hands, the morning mist and quiet broken by birds slanting toward water . . . and the thin, strange whistle of the wary drakes.

The morning of opening day his father had to come into his room and shake him awake. He knew it was three o'clock, but his mind was numb. Sitting on the edge of his bed, the boy had difficulty dressing himself in long underwear, khaki pants, and the red-plaid flannel shirt his mother had bought especially for the hunt. When he finally made his way into the fierce brightness of the kitchen, he found his father cooking pancakes, bacon, and fried eggs basted white with hot grease. His father was too busy to talk, and the boy was still half-asleep as they loaded decoys into the car's trunk and drove away from the house. Behind him from the back seat came the smells of leather and canvas gun cases, hunting coats, and the musty odor of his brother's hip boots.

It seemed to the boy that their Plymouth sedan was moving through an unfamiliar town, though he knew well an occasional landmark like the Petroleum Building and three tall hotels. Beyond the misty windshield, everything appeared shadowy and distorted. Soon the town dissolved into car lots, storage yards for well-servicing companies, auto courts, oilfield-equipment warehouses, and shabby honky-tonks. Eventually, the boy knew, there would be mile after mile of rolling grassland clumped with sagebrush and isolated trees, ranching country with cattle... and the lake.

Though the boy wanted to sleep, he felt it important to stay awake and appear alert to the drive. He suspected from his father's telephone conversations with other members of the duck club that he had decided just the two of them would drive together this morning, despite having only a B sticker for rationed gas. The boy was pleased by this, but also a little worried that he had been a disappointment to his father in complaining so strongly against Tom Ryan's becoming a new member of the club. He made a promise to himself that today he would make up for that by acting maturely around all his father's friends, including the men from the air base.

"Do you know what blind we'll be hunting in?" he asked.

"You and I are on the east side of the lake. It's a good spot and the blind's not bad—a long walk from the car, though."

"How about Sergeant Ryan? He'll be hunting in one of the blinds today, won't he?" His father glanced over at him, but the boy had expected that. "I don't mind," he said. "I was just wondering where he would hunt." It was, he knew, only partially true.

"He drew a blind on the west side, opposite us but clear across the lake. He'll have the sun in his eyes just after daybreak, but otherwise he and whoever hunts with him should do well."

"That's fine," the boy said, hoping to sound convincing. "Maybe everybody will get some good shooting." Then, though he knew it was probably pressing his luck too far, he added, "Carl must have really been disappointed about not getting home to hunt with us."

His father studied the road carefully. "Last year in Texas, Carl was getting tired of duck hunting. He was dating a lot and playing drums in that dance band with his friends. I think he was pretty fond of an older girl singing with them."

He had heard her name mentioned in conversations around the dinner table—Norma Jean or Nancy Jo, he thought. There was a shortage of musicians and the band had engagements every weekend. "Did he . . . want to marry her?"

"He may have for a while," his father said slowly. "They spent a good deal of time together with the band, and he was serious about her."

The boy could understand that part of it, his brother wanting to be with her and thinking seriously about her. But he wasn't sure what it had to do with not wanting to hunt. "Why didn't they get married?" he asked.

"He couldn't have supported a wife. Carl is going to college after the war, and it will be a long time before he can take care of a family. She probably wasn't the right girl anyway, though it took a while for him to accept that. He still hasn't gotten over her."

He wondered how one knew if a girl was right or wrong, but he did remember Carl staying shut up in his room after graduation and playing the same record, "Miss You," over and over. His parents had talked about Carl not being happy. But while they were fishing together on their vacation last summer, his brother had seemed all right. He hadn't acted upset about going into the Navy, either.

The boy sat up straighter on the car seat. "What happened to her . . . the girl he was serious about?"

"We heard she married a Marine Corps officer," his father said. "He was being reassigned to the Pacific."

He would have liked to hear more about his brother and the girl who had made him unhappy, but felt vaguely threatened by the story. He needed to think about it. It did make a difference, though, to learn Carl's feelings about hunting had changed, even though he wasn't sure whether his father saw his younger son as an inexperienced but available substitute. And the boy was certain that he would never lose his desire to hunt with his father. He would be different from Carl in that way, and it seemed to him a source of love and pride.

"Nothing means more to me than this hunt," he said, surprised at the tone of his voice.

His father reached over and gave his knee a quick, teasing squeeze with fingers that were thick and hard. He had worked as a roughneck on drilling rigs when starting out as a junior engineer, but the boy had no clear ambition, which sometimes worried him. His mother said no one could think clearly about the future while the war was going on.

"I hope it turns out to be a good morning," his father said. "Hell, if those refinished decoys don't produce, there's only one thing left for us to do."

The boy didn't understand that his father was joking. "What's that?" he asked.

"Cry, by god!" his father said, and after a moment the boy laughed too and felt terribly happy.

When they finally turned off the highway onto the dirt road which led to the lake, it was still dark. Soon, though, the boy saw a lighter streak of pale yellow to the east. Ahead of them the road dipped and began to climb, and then his father turned off, stopping before a padlocked gate leading through the barbed-wire fencing.

"Looks like we're the first ones here," his father said, when the boy climbed back into the car after relocking the gate behind them. "Hope nobody forgot their key this morning. It's a couple of miles more to where we park the car. Walking to the blind should warm us up a bit."

They finished the drive in silence. While his father unloaded the gunny sack filled with decoys, the boy fumbled with the unfamiliar hip boots before getting them fastened. Even with his hunting coat on he was cold and unable to move fast. He turned down the ear flaps on his cap and felt himself shaking as he uncased his shotgun. The wind shifted, and he smelled the lake for the first time—a damp, pungent odor of wet grass, mud, dying moss.

His father appeared beside him, seemingly unaffected by the cold as he assembled his over-and-under and stowed shells, a thermos, and sandwiches into his coat. He gave the boy his gun to carry and shouldered the heavy sack of decoys. Sky ahead of them had become lighter, with a thin stain of crimson edging the horizon below a widening wash of darker yellow. Carrying the two shotguns awkwardly, the boy followed the humped form ahead of him. Already his fingers were numb inside his gloves, but it was better now that they were moving.

To the boy's left was a huge black shape that slowly took on a glimmering surface as daylight increased. He heard the quiet slapping of water against the lake bank. His father stumbled in moving through uneven clumps of marsh grass. He swore and continued on without slowing down. Struggling to keep up, the boy wondered if he would be able to make it to the blind unless they stopped to rest. But he shifted the shotguns in his tired arms and kept going, his breath a great icy aching in his chest.

Eventually the boy gave up wishing for relief and plodded along mechanically like, he told himself, a tired soldier. He thought about how a fallen infantryman in magazine pictures became merely a dark, sprawling lump against sand, snow, or mud. One of his friends, whose brother had been killed in North Africa, said the dog tags were wedged between a dead soldier's teeth for identification, but the boy wasn't sure whether to believe him or not. No one he knew well had been killed in the war, though he still remembered being deeply moved by a story of Colin Kelly crashing his doomed B-17 into a Japanese battleship in the Philippines....

His father suddenly stopped. It had become light enough for the boy to make out the blind—a crude oblong of brush along the blurred edge of the lake.

"Are you all right?" his father asked. "It always seems a longer hike when you make it for the first time."

"I'm fine," he said, trying not to let his teeth chatter.

His father was pulling up his hip boots. "I'll set out the decoys while you're catching your breath." He took an armload from the sack and waded out into the water.

Soon the boy heard a splash as his father tossed a decoy into position before the blind. Realizing he should be useful, the boy lined up more decoys on the bank where his father could reach them easily. The sky behind him had become broken with red, and he heard a strange, sharp beating above him. The sound became fainter, receding into the distance. He had seen nothing of the ducks overhead, and their wings sounded much more powerful than he had expected, and he began to doubt his ability to hunt waterfowl as fast and clever as pintails, or the canvasbacks that his father said simply lowered their heads and flew faster when you shot at them. What if he should act foolishly when the actual shooting began and embarrass himself before his father? Even worse, he realized, would be his doing something stupid which might be noticed by his father's friends in the club... or by Sergeant Ryan in his blind across the lake.

As his father waded out with more decoys, the boy could hear the scrape of rowboat oars as a hunter at the upper end of the lake set out his blocks. A man began swearing somewhere to the west, his voice carried perfectly by the cold air. The words were coarse and surly, but the boy decided it didn't sound like Ryan.

By the time his father finished with the decoys, the sun was almost up, and they had to hurry into the blind and arrange the brush around them. The pit's bottom held a foot of icy water, but some old boards had been nailed into a crude bench. His father loaded the over-and-under and sat down. The boy did the same, and then attempted to imitate the way his father's eyes swept the sky from beneath the bill of his hunting cap. He found his own vision obscured by the cap or brush piled around the blind. Feeling awkward and unskilled, the boy sought an opening and looked out at the decoys. His breath caught when he saw them in early morning sunlight. Freshly painted and rolling with the motion of the water, they appeared to be real birds.

"They look perfect," he whispered.

His father nodded. "They're not bad. The proof, though, is whether they look right to the ducks."

The boy was about to say more, but realized he shouldn't be talking. Around them the sky had opened up into a clear light blue. It was still quite cold, and the boy had difficulty sitting still when his hips and feet were so uncomfortable. He stared at his shotgun and wondered if he would be able to move his arms to shoot. From the lower end of the lake came a double boom that echoed across the water, and he resisted the impulse to stand up and look in the direction of the shots. He waited, watching his father's face.

"Too high," his father said.

The boy had seen nothing. He stared again at the sun-brittle surface of the water. Across the lake he could see the brushy oblong of Ryan's blind against dry grass, but it was too far away to tell whether the pit was occupied. Secretly he hoped the sergeant might have forgotten his key and still be waiting by the locked gate for someone to come along and let him in. Or perhaps Ryan had not been allowed to leave the air base, or maybe, unlike Carl, he was being sent overseas into combat. The boy knew from news broadcasts and magazines that American fliers were making daylight raids over Germany, though the pictures in *Life* were often of some city viewed from above, with tiered bombs from Flying Fortresses or Liberators falling down like giant confetti. There wasn't any fighter protection for much of the flight, and the bombers were continually threatened by antiaircraft fire and attacked by Messerschmitts.

His father had said Sergeant Ryan was a radio operator and gunner in a bomber crew, and ever since the boy had seen Errol Flynn in *Dawn Patrol*, when he was much younger, he wanted to be a fighter pilot. But it might be better to have a chance of parachuting from a flaming B-24 bomber than to be shot down in to the sea like all the members of Torpedo Squadron Eight at the Battle of Midway. Although he had often visualized their old Devastator torpedo-bombers disappearing one by one as the Zeros attacked, he was unable to imagine beyond that point to the individual deaths of their crews in the cold water.

As he thought about Sergeant Ryan flying in combat, the face and voice of his wife became vivid in the boy's mind. He wished he could sit with her again and listen to her talk about herself, school, and the war. Even marriage ... the circumstances which brought her to a tiny garage apartment in an unfamiliar town surrounded by prairie and a strange sky where bombers circled away and back on training runs. When he talked with her again, he would tell her how the war troubled him, too, and that he would be her friend. At least he would want to say those things, and he wondered if she knew how he still felt her hair against his face and remembered the way light touched her eyes and skin....

"Keep down," his father said quietly. "I think they're mallards coming back for another look."

He couldn't see them without turning his face up into the light, but in a moment he heard their wings and then a faint gabble as some of them called to the silent decoys. His father slowly raised his duck call and blew a low-pitched feeding chuckle. The boy waited, straining his hearing to catch any sound from the sky. Then he heard again the stiff rustle of wings, closer this time than before.

"They circled back," said his father. "If they come into the decoys, I'll give the word. Pick a duck on your side and lay it on him."

The boy attempted to flex fingers clutching the shotgun like claws. He was having trouble getting enough breath. It seemed a long time ago that the ducks had first passed overhead. He decided something had gone wrong and wondered why his father was motionless beside him, the duck call dangling uselessly from the thong around his neck.

Then over the water near the decoys he saw ducks dropping in, their orange feet extended ... green heads of the males iridescent in sunlight ... blue swatches on the dark wings. He forgot everything and stared through the brush at the descending mallards as though it were his final vision of the world. And the ducks, a dozen or more, kept coming in, filling the boy's eyes with their shapes and movements.

"Now!" his father said sharply.

Somehow the boy stood up on his cramped legs. Instantly ducks backpedaled and flared, wings working bravely against the air. The boy was too absorbed in the moment to move quickly. His father swung his shotgun and fired once—a drake fell—and then again. A hen tumbled down into the lake among the decoys. Now the boy realized two mallards had come in to his left, and he pointed his shotgun, firing at the hen closest to the blind... and missing. Then almost like a dream he saw the drake rising into full flight and his gun barrel swinging up and ahead of the dark-green head as he fired, and the duck folding and falling through the sunlight, down... down into the heavy splash of water and his father pounding his back, the first duck he had ever killed and a clean shot. The air was tinted with the smell of burnt powder, and the ducks had vanished into blue sky.

His father grinned at him. "My god, I thought they were going to come right on in and knock our caps off!"

"I thought so too," the boy said. He laughed and fumbled around in his coat pocket for more shells. "I sure missed that hen, though. I missed her by about a mile."

And he wasn't nervous or even cold any longer.

Once inside the warm car, the boy felt his whole body relax. His father had poured him a final cup of luke-warm tea from his thermos, but the boy almost went to sleep holding the metal cup in both hands. He kept reliving parts of the hunt in his mind, like sunrise over the lake and the first ducks coming in to their decoys. During the morning he had shot two green-winged teal and a canvasback drake that flew straight over the blind, but it was the mallard he was most proud of, and he knew he would never forget that moment when it began to fall heavily from the sky above the lake and he became a hunter like his father.... He thought drowsily about the pair of pintails working over their decoys just before they quit hunting. It was strange that even his father had missed when the two drakes saw them at the last minute and flared off. In a way he wasn't sorry, for there were sure to be other hunts.

"A good day," his father said.

Later the boy remembered nodding and saying something about hoping they might hunt again the next weekend. But before they reached the highway, he had fallen asleep. When he woke up, their Plymouth was just entering town. It was a golden afternoon of fallen leaves and intense light, and they drove home through a residential section where boys tossed footballs across fading lawns shadowed by boxelders and poplars lining the street. The boy vaguely recalled homework he had promised his mother he would do as soon as he returned. He sat up.

"Will we take care of the ducks first thing?" he asked.

"That's right," his father said. "We can clean them in the back yard."

"I didn't think we would get so many the first time."

"Usually more ducks come down later in the season, when the weather gets worse. Probably we got lucky today."

The boy nodded, feeling very close to his father. "I'll have to clean my shotgun after supper. I could do yours too, if you like." He was hoping that his father would join him, the two of them working with hickory cleaning rods and Hoppe's solvent as they talked about the day's hunting.

"Thanks, Ray," his father said. "I may take you up on the offer. We've been having problems on one of the drilling rigs at Lance Creek. I'll have to make some phone calls and maybe drive up tomorrow to check things over. There was a blowout there last summer when they drilled into a gas pocket."

The boy remembered, for his father hadn't slept for several nights. After the funerals for the drilling crew, his mother had argued that he must see the doctor, but the boy wasn't sure he had gone. His father didn't like going to a doctor, and if he cut himself or didn't feel well, he would say, "I bruise easy and heal quick."

They turned into the driveway by the garage. The boy could see his mother waiting by the back door of the house, and he waved at her, trying to appear grown-up and energetic. If he wished to accompany his father on hunting trips, the boy knew he must show her that he hadn't gotten too tired and would be ready for school the next day. He began helping unload the decoys and then carried the two duck straps, heavy with game, into the yard.

"I'm glad you're both home," his mother said. She was wearing a fresh dress and apparently had fixed her hair while they were hunting. She seemed to the boy to be worried.

His father kissed her. "It's good to be back," he said and smiled tiredly.

"I hoped you wouldn't stay late," she said. "Did everything go all right? You didn't get too cold did you, Ray?"

His father laughed. "He's fine and we had a good hunt. We're a little hungry, though."

"Yes, I'm sure you are." She glanced absently through the screen door at a simmering pot on the range. "It's been a strange day.... Something terrible happened this morning and the news has been on the radio."

The war, the boy thought. It was something about the war. He knew it could have nothing to do with Carl, though. That was the lucky thing about his brother's being assigned to electronics school. He felt curious about what might have happened, and yet detached from his mother's concern. Nothing else seemed as important as the day's hunt.

"There was an accident early this morning out at the base," she said. "One of the bombers had engine trouble while starting to land and came down in the power lines along the highway."

"A bad one?" his father asked.

She was watching the boy. "The base commander said it was the worst so far. It burned.... The men didn't have a chance to get out."

His father shook his head. "It's a goddamned shame. I suppose the night practice is important."

"But there's something else about the crash," she said. "This afternoon on the radio . . . They were telling about the men and one of them, I think, was named Ryan. And I remembered that man in the duck club that you and Ray went to see. A sergeant, wasn't he?"

"That's right," his father said. "He was supposed to be hunting at the lake this morning, but no one was in the blind he drew. It could be a coincidence, though. I'd imagine several men named Ryan might be stationed at the base."

The boy left them talking on the steps and took his shotgun inside to the gun cabinet. It couldn't have been the sergeant he'd met who had been killed, he thought. No, it was someone else, someone less ugly and rude, probably without a wife at all. No.... But then, moving quickly, he went to the telephone in the hall and checked the phone book. After listening momentarily to be sure his parents were still outside, he lifted the receiver off the hook and asked the operator for the number. He waited, wondering how to begin, but determined to talk with her. The ringing continued, and then he heard the back door close and his mother's voice from the kitchen. He hung up.

"Your father told me you two had a fine day at the lake," his mother said as he passed her on the way outside.

"Yes, we did," he answered, trying to control his voice.

"You'll have to tell me all about it."

He was already at the door. "There isn't much to tell really. Everything went great." He smiled to reassure her, and she didn't press him further.

His father was laying out the birds. The boy watched his hands smoothing the breast feathers of each duck before placing it on the dying grass. "Thanks for taking me," he finally said.

His father nodded. "You did fine today, Ray. I should have realized earlier how much you wanted to hunt ducks this year. With the war going on, it's easy to forget how fast you're growing up."

The boy took a deep breath. "I understand, and it was dumb of me to act the way I did about Sergeant Ryan. I hope he..." He looked away, remembering his own thoughts of being a flier in the war, piloting a P-38 or P-40... even getting shot down in combat. But it hadn't occurred to him that death might come like this—some small mistake or mechanical failure, unexpected bad weather or distance misjudged, and your life ended. It could happen to him even now, to Carl on a plane flight to electronics school... or his father driving the company car up to the drilling site at Lance Creek tomorrow.

"I think it was probably Tom Ryan in the bomber that crashed," his father said. "It will be hard on his wife. When I get back in town, I'll see if she needs anything. Actually Ryan wasn't a bad sort of guy. He just talked like he was tough and knew everything."

"Maybe," the boy said uncertainly. "I guess I didn't know him very well. But if I was grown up and in the Air Corps, I wouldn't be like him."

"Are you sure, Ray? He was a whole lot older than you."

He had thought he was sure, but coming home from the hunt and hearing about the burning B-24 made the whole day different. Now after Carl was gone and he had proven his ability at the lake, it didn't seem right that he felt himself being tested again. From what his father had said that morning about Carl and his girlfriend, the boy realized his brother had grown up in ways he could only begin to understand. He wanted to share Carl's maturity, and he had become envious of Tom Ryan for being older, serving in the Air Corps, and having a wife with long shining hair and pale skin. But now, he thought, there is nothing to be jealous about.

His father stood up. "Sometimes being in the service and knowing what you'll be up against makes you act differently. I went through it myself in France, and I can begin to see it in Carl's letters. Most of the time you can't control what happens, and you have to do and see things that make you change. There's nothing romantic about fighting a war, Ray."

"I guess not," the boy said, knowing his father must be right but confused by images and words that he had grown up with—speeches, slogans, magazine advertisements, movies like *Air Force* and *Flying Tigers* with heroics he had relived in his imagination, the War Bond song on the radio. How could he know what was true or only an attractive illusion his immaturity accepted at face value? "Do you think I'll have to go?" he asked.

"I don't know," his father said quietly. "I hope not."

The sunlight had grown more brilliant as dusk approached. Feathers on the ducks shone in satiny patterns of warm color. The boy went on to the garage and began taking decoys from the wet sack, stacking them to dry on shelves along the wall. He had to rewind a few of the anchor cords, but the job was soon finished. The decoys had looked so natural riding the water in a long wedge before their blind. The shades of paint were duller than real feathers, but when wet the colors had tricked his eyes. He could understand how ducks would mistake the carved blocks for real mallards and pintails... and turn to pass lower over the water.

For a moment he wished he were still back at the lake... yet he doubted it would be the same now, with the sun falling and darkness eating at the cold water along the west shoreline. The hunters would all be gone and ducks would return, calling to those rafted up on the lake and circling empty blinds without fear. Suddenly the boy felt a terrible loneliness.... He was twelve and the war had been going on somewhere since he was eight years old. Already he was beginning to miss Carl. It could be weeks before his father was able to take him hunting again, and even then it might not be the same at all. Everything could change right before one's eyes like the fading colors of sunrise or water being touched by wind and shadow.

The boy left the garage and tried to find his father, but there was no one in the yard. He stood by the dead ducks and looked toward the house. Through a kitchen window he could see his father and mother standing together with their arms around one another. When he thought about trying to make the telephone call to Ryan's wife, he only felt more alone... and frightened of himself. She might not even remember him, and his clumsy words could have revealed his own hope for acceptance, rather than the comfort he wanted to give her. His face burned with embarrassment and longing, and there was nothing he could do to bring back the feeling of perfect happiness he had known earlier that afternoon when remembering the hunt.

After a while Ray took out his pocketknife and knelt by the ducks. The evening had started to cool and he tried to work fast. Above him, through almost-bare cottonwoods, the sky shifted from blue to gray, with touches of orange smearing the underside of clouds. He shivered and pulled at the tough, slippery insides of the mallard drake he had shot. Ray thought of its fall through sunlight into the quiet water and the two pintails gracefully flaring away from his blind as the hunt ended. There would be other mornings. His hand was red. But the blood dried quickly against his skin.

ABOUT ROBERT RORIPAUGH

Robert Roripaugh was appointed by Governor Jim Geringer to serve as Wyoming Poet Laureate from 1995 through 2002. A writer of fiction as well as poetry, he grew up in California, West Texas, and Wyoming, where he ranched with his parents along the Wind River Mountains west of Lander. Roripaugh completed B.A. and M.A. degrees at the University of Wyoming. After Army service in Japan, he came back to UW as a Coe Fellow in American Studies and did further graduate work at the University of New Mexico. For thirty-five years he taught Creative Writing and Western American Literature at the University of Wyoming.

Stories and poems by Robert Roripaugh have been widely published in magazines, journals, and anthologies, including *The Atlantic, Quarterly West, South Dakota Review, Higher Elevations: Stories from the West, Anthology of Magazine Verse and Yearbook of American Poetry, Poets West,* and *Deep West: A Literary Tour of Wyoming.* His poetry is collected in *Learn to Love the Haze* and *The Ranch,* which was a finalist in the Western Writers of America Spur Awards for 2002. Roripaugh's novel set in postwar Japan, *A Fever for Living,* was published in the United States and England. *Honor Thy Father,* a historical novel about a family ranching in the Sweetwater River country, received a Western Heritage Award (the Wrangler) from the National Cowboy Hall of Fame and in 2004 was reprinted in a paperback edition by HarperCollins.

Roripaugh frequently gives readings, workshops, and talks on Wyoming Literature. His writing and career are the subject of a booklet by John D. Nesbitt, published in 2004 as part of Boise State University's Western Writers Series. Roripaugh lives in Laramie with his wife, Yoshiko, and continues to write about Wyoming and the West.

The text is composed in twelve-point Garamond by Adobe.
Display type is Cyan created by the Wilton Foundry.
The book is printed on Nature's Natural,
an acid free, recycled paper,
by
Thomson-Shore.

High Plains Press is committed to preserving ancient forests and natural resources. We elected to print *The Legend Of Billy Jenks* on 50% post consumer recycled paper, processed chlorine free. As a result, for this printing, we have saved:

7 trees (40' Tall and 6-8" Diameter)
3,061 Gallons of Wastewater
1,231 Kilowatt Hours of Electricity
337 Pounds of Solid Waste
663 Pounds of Greenhouse Gases

High Plains Press made this paper choice because our printer, Thomson-Shore, Inc., is a member of Green Press Initiative, a nonprofit program dedicated to supporting authors, publishers, and suppliers in their efforts to reduce their use of fiber obtained from endangered forests.

For more information, visit www.greenpressinitiative.org